Sand Dweller

Molly Neely

Sand Dweller

Copyright © 2023 – Molly Neely

This book is a work of Fiction. Any references to historic events, real people, or real places are used fictitiously. Other names, characters, places, and events are the products of the author's imagination. Any resemblance to actual events, places or persons (living or dead), is entirely coincidental.

All Rights Reserved – No part of this book may be reproduced or transmitted in any form without written permission of the author.

Paperback ISBN: 978-1-952796-17-3

Published by:
Cloaked Press, LLC
PO Box 341
Suring, WI 54174
Cloakedpress.com

Dedication

For my Lord and Savior, Yeshua. Who took the sins and burdens of this world upon His shoulders, destroyed them with His death and renewed them with His Resurrection. To You, all Honor and Glory, now and forever.

CONTENTS

Chapter 1 1

Chapter 2 5

Chapter 3 11

Chapter 4 15

Chapter 5 19

Chapter 6 23

Chapter 7 29

Chapter 8 37

Chapter 9 43

Chapter 10 51

Chapter 11 59

Chapter 12 65

Chapter 13 69

Chapter 14 73

Chapter 15 79

Chapter 16 85

Chapter 17 89

Chapter 18 93

Chapter 19 99

Chapter 20 105

Chapter 21 111

Chapter 22 117

Chapter 23 123

Chapter 24 131

Chapter 25 139

Chapter 26 147

Chapter 27 153

Chapter 28 157

Chapter 29 163

Chapter 30 167

Chapter 31 173

Chapter 32 177

Chapter 33 183

Chapter 34 189

Epilogue 193

Acknowledgments.. 195

Chapter 1

"Well, I think that's enough for today," Father Caleb said. "I think you have a lot to meditate on, Bob. Let's schedule another session for two weeks, and see how you're doing, okay?"

Bob wrung his hands nervously. "You really think I need to come back?"

Caleb smiled. "You have been struggling with alcoholism for a lot of years, Bob. You can't expect to be totally cured after one session with a priest."

"Yeah, b—but—" Bob stammered.

"No buts," Caleb said. "You've developed a destructive habit over the years. It's going to take more than an hour to break it."

Father Caleb scooted his chair closer to his charge and extended his hands.

"Come on. Let's pray," he said.

Bob gave a slight nod and took Caleb's hands in his. For several moments, the room was silent, save the quiet ticking from a wall clock that hung over the door.

Caleb took in several deep breaths, waiting for the right words to come to mind. But there was nothing. Panic began to set in. Why was his mind a complete blank? Caleb's breathing grew shallow as he tried to pick his brain for a word, a psalm, anything to offer in prayer, but he found himself to be at a complete loss.

He opened his eyes and scanned the walls of the office for some visual inspiration. As his eyes fell on the large bookcase behind Bob, a scratching sound grabbed his attention. Caleb let go of Bob's hands and stood up. Cautiously, he walked to the bookcase and peered into the small, dark spaces between the books.

A high-pitched shriek pierced the air, as a small winged creature leapt out from behind a row of dusty pew Bibles, clawing Caleb's face.

"Son of a—" Caleb cursed, clutching his cheek. He pulled his hand away and looked. Blood.

The creature perched itself on the sill of an open window and hissed, releasing a cloud of sulfuric stench into the room.

"What in God's name are you?" Caleb whispered, crossing himself.

Repelled by the gesture, the creature turned its head, moaning as if in pain. Then it jumped from the sill, knocking over a small potted fern, and flew straight at Caleb.

As the creature darted past Caleb's head, he swung his arms wildly, trying to swat the beast out of the air.

Like a buzzing fly, the creature U-turned in mid-air and took one more pass at Caleb, before bee-lining for the open window. It hovered there for a moment, cocking its dog-like head to one side, as if sizing up Caleb for another attack.

Caleb stood motionless in the center of the room, his hand clutching the edge of his desk. Looking down, he spied his letter opener. Quickly he grabbed it then pointed it at the creature.

"Be gone, devil." His voice trembled.

The creature let out another ear-piercing shriek then darted out the window.

Bob's eyes remained closed, pressed together with desperate resolve, waiting to hear God's words of encouragement flow from the lips of his priest. A small bead of sweat formed on his temple and slowly traced a thin line down the side of his face. Distracted by the feeling, Bob brushed the perspiration away with his shoulder. Then he frowned.

"Are you waiting for something, Father?" Bob asked.

Father Caleb opened his eyes. Still seated across from his charge, he looked around the room in confusion. Everything was in its proper place, even the fern was resting comfortably on the window ledge.

"Uh, no," Caleb said finally, "We're sitting in quiet meditation. Focus all of your attention on the Lord, Bob. When He gives you inspiration, go ahead and just speak out."

Bob nodded, gripping Caleb's hands tighter.

"Holy Lord," Bob called out. "Help me with this burden. I feel so weak against the desire to fill myself with booze. Because of it, I am failing as a husband, I'm failing at my job, and my kids are afraid of me. Lord, send down Your Holy Spirit, to reinforce my soul. To give me the power and authority to banish this sin from my life, once and for all. In Jesus Name, Amen."

"Amen," Father Caleb echoed. "It's good that you took the lead. Christ wants you to reach out to Him. How do you feel?"

Bob stood up and stretched. "Pretty good, actually."

Caleb glanced around nervously as he rose and shook Bob's hand. "I want you to offer prayers to God every day," he said, "No matter how busy you are. Check in with Him, even if you're feeling strong, and don't forget to call that eight-hundred number I gave you. Alcoholics Anonymous will provide you with tons of support. I'll see you in two weeks."

Bob grabbed up his jacket from the back of his chair and started for the door. He reached for the knob then turned back around. "Thank you, Father," he said, "Oh, and you might want to close that window. There's a bad smell coming in from outside."

Caleb quickly went to the open window, his eyes darting back and forth, searching for the creature. Satisfied that it was nowhere in sight, he closed the window. "There," he said with a weak smile. "I'll have to ask my secretary to bring me an air freshener. See you in two weeks?"

"Yes, you will," Bob answered with a chuckle. "And thank you again, Father Caleb."

When Bob was gone, Caleb's ran his hand across his cheek. He could still feel the sting of the creatures claws, yet somehow the wound had vanished. He walked back over to the window one last time and looked out. The blue sky peeked shyly through the trees that bordered the courtyard outside his office.

"Lord, what just happened?" he asked.

The only answer he got was the steady ticking from the wall clock.

CHAPTER 2

Scorching winds whipped through the plains, spreading clouds of dust and soul debris across the landscape of Hell. She stared silently out the window, listening to the maddening screams of the damned. There was almost a melody in their cries, a haunting symphony of agony and despair.

She often wondered what would have happened if her children were the one's walking the Earth instead of the Sons of Eve. A sudden pang of jealousy ripped through her stomach. How she hated that weak-willed woman and her squandering offspring. A speck of soul dust found its way into her eye. Instantly a tear squeezed its way from her ducts, only to evaporate in the dense heat. She grew weary of the torrid fires and constant hopelessness. The Most High had given her paradise then ripped it all away. As punishment for refusing to be Adam's wife, the Lord had banished her to Hell.

Turning away from the window, she wandered around her chamber, gazing upon its gray stone walls. Walking past her small bedside table, she lovingly caressed the one treasure she had—a small ornately carved black box, made from charred human bone. A trophy won in secret, she had stolen it right out from under the demon's nose. She considered it payment, after all, she was not content to be

Hell's plaything for free.

An ear-piercing shriek from the ground below grabbed her attention. Walking back to the window, she looked down just in time to see one of Lucifer's nephilim devour the guts from a soul. Once the children of angels, these horribly deformed creatures now scoured the plains of Hell searching for the damned to prey on. The way they tore at the soul's flesh, ripping at the remains of a fallen man, was enough to reduce the bravest warrior to the yellowest of cowards. The descent into Hell was equally tragic. Some souls were so badly destroyed that, by the time they landed, there was almost nothing left.

"So pitiful," she murmured to herself in disgust. "the Sons of Eve are weak!" she shouted out the window. The gorging nephilim paused to look up at her for a moment then bit the head off the soul. "You are all pathetic!" she called out.

"Such passion," a voice groaned from behind her. "You must have forgotten our appointment."

She cringed at the sound of the voice. She knew all too well what day it was. Azazael never missed his appointments with her. He was the demon she most hated—and most feared. Azazael was well renowned as the first demon to denounce the humans. It didn't matter to Azazael that she wasn't really mortal anymore. Whenever he came to her chambers, she knew it meant hours of suffering. Not because he beat her or used her for sexual perversion as some did. Azazael was one of the few demons who didn't. No, it was his endless mind games she hated.

She turned and faced her unwelcome guest. Without

hiding her disgust, she bowed and replied, "What is your bidding today?"

"Oh, Lilith, my precious toy," he hissed seductively. "Why do you always assume I want something?" Azazael paused, licking his lips. "Is it so hard to believe that I simply desire to be in your presence?" He smiled as he walked around her, sizing up his prey. "I am beginning to think, perhaps, you do not like it when I visit."

Facing her, Azazael hunched down so his eyes were level with Lilith's. He grabbed her by the shoulders and pressed her to his chest. The bony armor he wore cut into her cheek.

"Lilith, can you not feel the desperate beating of my heart?" Laughing, he shoved her down hard onto the stone floor.

"You have no heart, demon!" she growled through clenched teeth. "Why do you plague me with torment? Are there not enough humans for you to pester on the surface?"

"Precious toy," Azazael replied, "this is why I enjoy your company. You always give the most flattering compliments."

Walking over to a large stone chair, he sat down. Then leaning forward onto his knees, Azazael smiled. "Today is going to be a special day for you," he said. "Your soul is crying, and I desire to ease your pain."

"You know nothing of me," Lilith said, standing up. "much less, my soul."

"What if I told you that you could leave Hell, tonight?" Azazael said evenly. "If I could make that happen, how grateful would you be?"

The delight was hard for Lilith to hide. But she was nobody's fool. Cautiously, she took a few steps towards the demon. "What do you mean, leave?" she asked. "What is in it for you?"

"Do you not trust me?" he asked "Is it so hard to believe that I simply want to give you a gift—" Azazael paused. "—for centuries of *loyal* service." His eyes glimmered red, waiting for her to respond.

"So my gift from you is freedom?" Lilith asked, frowning.

"Freedom is part of it," Azazael winked. "and I want to give you a child."

Lilith threw her head back and burst into laughter. "You must be joking! I would never allow you to sire a child in my womb!"

In a flash, Azazael stood, marched across the room and grabbed her by the throat. "Proud, selfish human," he snarled, "after all these centuries, you still think you are superior to me? The Most High tossed you from Eden like a useless pile of refuse! Compared to me, you are as weak as a lamb. Do you think you could prevent me from tearing your body to shreds if it pleased me to do so?"

Sulfuric smoke blasted from his nostrils. Azazael released his hold on her for a moment, then pulled Lilith close, draping his arms around her like a lover. "I am proposing a wager," he whispered, stroking her long black hair. "Let us each go and breathe life into a child."

Lilith pulled away and glared at Azazael. "I am listening," she said.

"Our offspring will test their merit against one another on the field of battle," he said, slowly. "If your child is the victor, neither I nor any other demon will ever darken your door again."

Lilith nervously twisted a piece of her hair around her finger. "And?" she demanded.

"And," Azazael replied, "if my child is found victorious, you will submit to me, body and soul, *forever*."

Lilith shook her head. "No. Lucifer would never allow me to leave Hell. And The Most High, what of Him? It is forbidden for me to walk the Earth!"

Azazael began to retreat towards the chamber door. "Have you not heard? The Most High has granted mankind free will."

Lilith's heart began to quicken. A wave of hope flooded her veins. Her eyes scanned the chambers she had occupied for so long. She shuttered at the thought of the endless atrocities she had been a party to in those rooms. Freedom. It was too hard to resist. Looking down at the floor, Lilith contemplated all that Azazael had said. "What are the odds," she said quietly, "that Lucifer would just let me go?"

"Precious toy," Azazael said smiling, "let us go and ask him."

CHAPTER 3

The walk to Lucifer's chambers was long and silent. Lilith had never been in the south wing of the palace. Reserved for the most illustrious guests, the dark lord's private wing held an air of mystery and dread. Lilith glanced up and stared in awe at the chandeliers that hung from the high vaulted ceilings. Each one was constructed from of dozens of human skeletons, positioned in the most graphic sexual positions. Candles protruded from the mouths of the skulls, the thick gray wax running down their jaws, adding another macabre layer to an already troubling display.

Lilith's legs cramped from the strain of trying to keep up with Azazael's quick pace. When they finally reached the door of the dark prince, Lilith could feel her heart freeze in her chest. Azazael knocked twice, then ushered Lilith in, shutting the mammoth stone door behind them. The sound of the latch on the door jump started her heart once more and, as Lilith glanced around the private chambers of the undisputed king of Hell, she began to think she had made a terrible mistake.

"My brother, we have come to seek your blessing," Azazael said, bowing deeply. "Will you hear our request?"

Lucifer sat before them, his hands folded atop a large stone desk. Once the most beautiful and wise of the

Heavenly Host, it was Lucifer's ego that was damaged the most by his fall. Lilith marveled at how much of his beauty was still intact. His raw sexuality made her weak in the knees. But at the same time, like the rest of Hell's residents, she feared his evil more than she desired his affections.

"Come closer, brother." Lucifer beckoned. "I have many moments to spare for you."

With his hand firmly clasped around the back of Lilith's neck, Azazael motioned her closer to Lucifer. "We, Lilith and I, would like your permission to go up to the surface." Azazael paused. The faintest of smiles lifted the corners of his mouth then quickly disappeared. "I have challenged her to a duel, so to speak."

Lucifer raised an eyebrow, his interest clearly piqued. "What kind of duel?"

"It is my claim that, if we were to both sire children on the surface and those children were to face each other in battle, that my offspring would be victorious," Azazael proclaimed, puffing his chest out proudly.

Lucifer pushed his chair back and rose. Hands clasped behind him, the dark lord walked around the desk and stood in front of Lilith. He reached out and grabbed her chin, tilting her face upward. "And what say you about this claim, fallen human?"

"I—" she stuttered nervously. "I am confident that the fruit of my womb will win the day, my lord."

He released his grip on Lilith's face and chuckled. "Such pride," he mused, returning to his chair, "sounds to me that you only desire an excuse to leave this paradise I have made for you. If that is the case, then I must deny your request."

Azazael opened his mouth to protest, but Lucifer raised his hand. "Say nothing, my brother." he warned.

Lilith flung herself to the floor, arms outstretched in submission. "Please, my lord!" she begged, "I swear to you, I will sire a mighty warrior for your armies! Allow me to prove my loyalty."

The dark prince glanced over at Azazael. The demon returned his gaze and nodded once. "Very well," Lucifer said with a sigh. "But there will be conditions. Never forget, I am master over all the Earth. I alone hold the influence and power over man. So neither of you will maintain any contact with your children after they are born. I cannot have you corrupting their little minds."

Lilith stood up and bowed to Lucifer. "Oh thank you, gracious lord!" she exclaimed. She flashed a victorious grin at Azazael then bolted from Lucifer's chambers.

"What is the *real* reason for this wager, my brother?" Lucifer asked. "Surely you have better things to occupy your time with."

Azazael reached into his cloak and produced a small black box. His face filled with sorrow as he caressed the box, turning it over in his hands. "Do you still dream of our time Above?" he asked.

"No," Lucifer snapped. "And I am surprised that you do. What does that have to do with the fallen human, Lilith?"

"This box is made from the bones of my human wife, the only human ever worthy of my love," Azazael said. "After we fell, I was able to locate her soul. I keep it in this box, that way I can keep her safe." Azazael turned and started for the door. "That filthy human stole my wife. I found her in Lilith's chamber. She will not keep her end of the bargain, of that I am certain. In fact, I am counting on it." He opened the door then stood there motionless for a few seconds.

"What is it, brother?" Lucifer called out.

Without looking back, Azazael replied, "I am just anxious to make that whore pay for her treachery."

CHAPTER 4

2489 B.C., Egypt

The blackness of the night descended upon the pharaoh like death itself. Once again, he would endure another sleepless evening, as he had for months. Userkaf, Pharaoh of Egypt, lived with the constant fear that his gods would curse the land and his people with it. The high priests had read all of the signs and had come to the same conclusion: The pharaoh needed an heir.

Every girl in the empire of breeding age had been brought before the pharaoh. The palace cooks stuffed him daily with aphrodisiacs from all over the known world. Hours a day were spent meditating and praying to Min and Isis for fertility. But, in spite of all his vigorous efforts, Userkaf still had no son to take his place.

He lounged on his bed in silence, listening to the light breeze blowing outside his window. The cool night air was a small relief from the nervous sweats that plagued him. Suddenly, the sweet scent of blue lotus blossoms began to fill the room, faintly at first, then growing thick and stifling.

The pharaoh sat up and looked around, confused. Blue lotus only bloomed in the morning sun. A mixture of fear and anger swept over him. "Who is there?" Userkaf called out. "I can smell your perfume. Show yourself to me at once!" Drifting in from the window, he heard the faintest of laughs.

A delicate hand parted the sheer silk draperies that hung above the windows. "I know what your heart desires, great king." A beautiful woman stepped out from behind the draperies. "It beats with an untamed hunger. That is why I have come to you."

Userkaf was entranced by her. He watched as the woman leapt like a cat from the window ledge down to the floor. Her naked body, glistening in the moonlight, gave her skin the look of polished silver. The pharaoh was suddenly filled with dread. Something was wrong with his body. His forehead broke out in a layer of sweat, that instantly began to crawl its way down the side of his face. Panic gripped his heart. Everything inside him was screaming to bolt from the room, but the king found that he was unable to move.

She made her way to the foot of the bed then grabbed the bed clothes and pulled them off the terrified pharaoh. Seeing that Userkaf himself was totally unclothed, the woman smiled. "Mmmm, I see you were expecting me," she said slyly. The woman climbed up onto the bed, straddling the naked pharaoh. Userkaf gasped with fear. "You see," she said, pressing him deep into her body. "I have a proposition for you."

Userkaf's mind was reeling. Why was his body cooperating? "What is it that you want, devil?" he whispered.

"I want a child, great king," the woman moaned, "and

you need an heir to the throne." Leaning forward, the woman gently kissed him, pushing her tongue into his mouth. "By this night's end, we will both have what we desire."

Userkaf shook his head defiantly. "No, this is wrong," he gasped. "release me from your spell. It is I who should be taking you, not the other way around."

The woman's eyes, a glittering shade of green, suddenly washed over with blackness. "Fool!" she spat. "No man *takes* me. I can have any mortal I desire, be grateful that I have chosen you."

Arching her back, the woman began to grind against the pharaoh. Though his mind was filled with terror, Userkaf's body gave in to the pleasure, thrusting his manhood into the enchanted woman.

Within moments, the pharaoh gave up his seed. Instantly, the woman climbed off the king and began to walk back toward the window.

"Wait!" Userkaf called out. "Where are you going? What of the child you promised? I do not even know your name, or how to find you!"

The woman stopped at the window ledge and turned to face the pharaoh. "Do not fear, great king. I will not leave the palace. As for the child, *he* will grow up in the house of his father. You should congratulate yourself, nine months from tonight, I will give birth to a god, and you will have your heir."

Userkaf continued to lie motionless and confused as the woman climbed up onto the ledge. "And your name?" he asked.

"My name is Lilith," the woman replied, "of Eden."

In an instant, Lilith turned and jumped out of the window. With Lilith gone, the pharaoh felt the control of his body return to him. Userkaf leapt from his bed and bolted to the window. But when he looked out, all he found was the night sky and the scent of blue lotus lingering on the breeze.

CHAPTER 5

Azazael stood silently in the corner of the tent, staring at the young girl for what seemed like hours. Her slow, hypnotic breathing, the smooth, firm texture of her face and the way her wavy onyx hair spilled across her shoulders, seemed to cast a spell of its own on the demon. He had not anticipated such a reaction at the sight of the sleeping girl. Azazael had ravaged many human women over the ages, and none had ever brought out any deep emotions in him. After the fall and the death of his one and only love, Azazael afforded himself nothing but contempt for the daughters of Eve. Perhaps it was her youth, that brought about such feelings of longing and sorrow. His wife had not been much older than this girl when she died. The guilt had been burning a hole in his heart for centuries. Whatever it was, as soon as he chose her, Azazael knew what he had to do.

Reaching into his cloak, Azazael pulled out his black box. With shaking hands, he unfastened the latch and opened the lid.

"My dearest," he called out softly. "I will not create a life with any other but you. Come."

A faint sound echoed from inside the box. Gathering his strength, Azazael crossed the tent and set the open box beside the girl.

"Arise from your eternal slumber, my love," he whispered again. "If only for a moment, reside in the body of this woman, so that I may once again feel the warmth of your touch."

A soft green glowing mist began to creep out of the box, and found its way into the sleeping girl's nostrils. At once, the young woman's eyes opened and she sat up.

"Husband," she called out, "do I live again?"

Azazael sat down beside her. "Only for this night, my dearest. Do not waste time with words. We will let our love speak for us."

Taking her in his arms, Azazael kissed her with a thousand years of suppressed desire. Quickly their clothes were shed, and when he entered her, the young woman cried out.

"What is it, my dearest?" Azazael asked, with worry.

"This body is pure, husband," she gasped. "A woman's first time is often painful."

The discovery that his wife's host was a virgin made him want her even more. His memories drifted back to their wedding night, as slowly, Azazael began to work himself in and out with steady, gentle movements. His heart ached with a luxury he had not allowed himself to feel in centuries, love. When the pressure and emotions could no longer be contained, the demon came with a deep groan.

Afterward, they lay in each other's arms, soaking up every moment they had together. It was as if the lovers had never been separated. But as dawn began to approach, Azazael's heart grew heavy. His time with his bride had to come to an end.

Leaving her on the bed, Azazael stood up and dressed. When he turned back to face her, his heart broke at the sight of her tears.

"Oh, my husband, must this night end?" she sobbed. "After all this time apart, how can you ask me to leave you now? More than ever I fear I cannot live without you!"

Azazael said nothing. Reaching down to the floor, he retrieved the black box. With tears welling in his eyes, Azazael held the box out to her.

"Will I see you again, husband?" she asked.

Azazael nodded. "The fallen human, Lilith, is the only one in Hell, who lives body and soul. If all goes according to my plans, you will soon have a permanent host, and we will finally be together for eternity. That is my promise to you, my love."

She gave him a knowing smile and silently leaned back onto the bed. Instantly, the glowing mist, rushed out from the girl's mouth and back into the box.

"Awan," a voice suddenly called from outside the tent. "Are you awake, child?"

Quickly, Azazael tucked the box back into his cloak and vanished into the shadows as the flaps of the tent opened.

"Awan! It is time to rise, girl. The grain does not grind itself!"

Awan opened her eyes and glanced over at the old woman standing at the entrance of her tent.

"Forgive me," Awan said with a yawn. "I will be there to help you in a few moments."

Muttering, the old woman turned on her heel and stormed out of the tent. Awan shook her head, threw off her bed clothes, and stood up. At once, a searing pain tore through her groin. Her knees buckled and Awan fell back onto the bed. Then a nervous flutter entered her stomach. Cautiously Awan reached down between her legs. A knot boiled up in her throat as she pulled her hand out and saw the strange mixture of blood and fluid on her fingertips. Awan's mother had schooled her in the ways of marriage, before she died. She had not wanted her only daughter to be unprepared on her wedding night. Awan knew instantly from those teachings what had happened. Her virginity, somehow, had been stolen in the night.

"But by whom?" she whispered aloud. "Surely I would have awakened."

Awan sat on her bed for a few more moments, desperately trying to sort out her predicament. But the screeching voice of the old woman brought Awan out of her thoughts.

"I am coming!" she called out, scrambling around for her sandals.

As she pulled back the flap of her tent, Awan took one last look around her dwelling, hoping that a clue to her mystery could be seen. But, there was nothing. Letting out a deep breath, Awan walked out into the freshness of the morning, hoping it was just a bad dream.

CHAPTER 6

2488 B.C., Sinai Desert

"We accuse Awan, daughter of Tobias, elder of the Bedouin tribe of Sinai, of fornication with demons, resulting in the birth of an unholy child!"

The words stung Awan's ears. Only twenty four hours had passed since she had given birth, but her father, Tobias, and the rest of the tribes' elders made that time feel like an eternity.

A few months after that terrible morning in her tent, Awan began to notice changes in her body. When six months had gone by, her worst fears were confirmed and it was clear she could no longer hide her condition. She remembered the deep pain and anger in her father's eyes when she told him. She also remembered the welts he left on her back.

The only mercy Tobias had allowed his daughter was that she wouldn't be stoned. But he had insisted that punishment had to be given in some form, and the day of atonement had finally arrived.

"It is our submission," the elder continued, "that a trial by ordeal is the only way to determine whether or not she has compromised her morals."

Awan's eyes grew wide with fear. A trial by ordeal was seldom used, especially with women. The elders were going to let Yahweh decide. Awan raised her eyes up to the sky. Silently she prayed that the Lord would grant justice and mercy to her and her child.

"Very well," Tobias said. Turning to a small middle-aged man standing among the tribe, Tobias asked, "Theudas, you are Muktar of this tribe. Are you prepared to judge in this matter?"

Theudas bowed to the elders, and replied, "I am."

He stepped forward and took his place next to Tobias and the other elders. Awan watched nervously as an Orfi was chosen to mediate the trial, and a Mubesha to witness it. When Theudas had chosen the men he needed for the trial, he sat down in front of the ceremonial fire.

"Bring the accused woman forward," he said in a stony voice.

Awan was ushered passed the elders and placed in front of the fire, across from Theudas.

"Since no man of this tribe has come forward to claim the child as his, you have been accused of fornicating with demons," he said evenly. "You have denied this claim, and we have found no witnesses to testify against you. For this reason, we will perform a Bisha'a. The Lord will be your judge. To *not* accept, is to admit guilt. Do you accept?"

Awan nodded, her hands trembling. "The Lord will give me justice," she said, her eyes meeting his. "I am ready."

Theudas stood and walked around to face Awan. Then, reaching down, he picked up a small knife whose blade had been resting in the coals. He held it up for all to see, drawing gasps from the crowd. Awan turned away for a moment, the glow of the hot blade turning her stomach.

"If you, Awan, daughter of Tobias, are innocent of the crimes leveled against you, this hot blade will not scorch your tongue. Then we will know that you speak the truth, and that Yahweh has declared you innocent."

Awan closed her eyes and opened her mouth. Theudas carefully laid the flat knife blade down on her tongue. Awan opened her eyes and frowned at Theudas. He returned her gaze with a puzzled look, but said nothing. After several minutes, it became clear that the blade was not burning her tongue.

Removing the hot knife from Awan's mouth, Theudas asked, "Why did you not cry out? Did the heat from the metal not burn on your tongue?"

"No," she replied, as tears rimmed her eyelids, "the Lord has answered my prayers. The blade felt as cold as the winter winds."

The crowd erupted in shouts of joy. Theudas motioned for the Orfi and Mubesha to step forward and inspect Awan's tongue. When the two men looked inside her mouth, they found no trace of burns anywhere. Then they inspected the knife, and found that it was still glowing from the heat of the fire. Satisfied, Theudas turned and faced the elders.

"Yahweh has declared this woman, Awan, daughter of Tobias, innocent of fornication," he said in a loud voice. "Thanks be to God, who is a righteous judge."

Theudas looked back at Awan and nodded. "You are free to return to your life."

Awan walked across the clearing to her father, and

stood before him. "Father," she said in a low voice, "I am happy that your honor is still intact."

Tobias stood staring at her for a moment then grabbed at the two sides of his robe and tore them. The tribe, that had been celebrating Awan's innocence, stopped and stared in disbelief.

"You speak to me of honor?" he screamed. "My daughter, who breeds with devils, would dare to speak to me of honor?"

"But, Father, I—" Awan began.

Tobias's hand shot out and slapped his daughter across the cheek. "Whore of Satan!" he spat. "You may have fooled this tribe, the witnesses, even that naive Theudas, but not me!" Tobias pushed her aside and marched over to Theudas. "And you!" he growled. "What of the child? He is not welcome in my tents! Surely you do not intend for this judgment to extend to him as well?"

"The Lord has handed down his verdict, Tobias," Theudas said. "Who are you to question the Lord? If the mother is spared, so is the child."

"This cannot be!" Tobias yelled.

"It is not for you to decide!" Theudas fired back. "This child may be a blessed gift from God Himself!"

"He may also be a curse spat up from Hell!" Tobias exclaimed. "Do not forget, *no* man has come forward to claim him. It is more likely that he is the son of a demon, than a blessing from Heaven."

Tobias paced like an enraged animal around the fire. Minutes crawled by like hours, as the tribe waited for him to speak again.

"Theudas," he said finally, "I stand behind my good

opinion. My daughter may return to my tents, but the child is not welcome." Tobias paused for a moment then continued. "Take him into the wilderness. Let the buzzards pick his carcass."

"No, Father, please!" Awan cried.

"Yes," he shouted back, "you have no say in this matter."

"Tobias," Theudas said suddenly, "I will solve this problem for you." Turning to Awan, he said, "Woman, go and get your child. Bring him to me."

Awan ran to her tent and quickly retrieved her son. A few moments later, she returned and handed the small baby over to Theudas's waiting arms.

"Since this child is not welcome in your tents," Theudas said carefully to Tobias, "I will raise him myself."

"Fool, Theudas." Tobias laughed. "You would soil our tribe with a devil's spawn?"

"No, I would not," Theudas answered. "You have left me no choice, Tobias. For the sake of the community, I will take a Nazarite Vow and leave with the child."

"You cannot—" Tobias started.

One of the elders stepped forward. "Tobias, it is the law. If he wishes to take the vow, you cannot stop him."

"After his circumcision, the child and I will leave," Theudas said, "and you, Tobias, can stand alone with your good opinion."

Enraged, Tobias stormed back to his tents surrounded by the whispers of a shocked crowd.

"Awan," Theudas said.

"Yes?" she replied, shyly.

"Yahweh has a plan for your child, and I will see to it

that it is fulfilled," he said. "Have you chosen a name for your son?"

Staring embarrassed at the ground, Awan shrugged. "Well, uh…no," she said.

"Then, we shall name him Malachi, Ben Sinai."

Awan tilted her head slightly and gave Theudas a quizzical look. "Why that name?"

"It means, messenger of God." he answered.

CHAPTER 7

2470B.C., Sinai Desert

Theudas stood, legs apart, his arms outstretched, waiting for the attack. Sweat beaded on his old weathered brow, streaking the layers of dust that had settled on his face.

"I wonder, my son," he pondered, "are you are ever going to master these moves?"

Malachi crouched in front of the old man, like a young lion waiting to pounce. Then with lightning quickness, he lunged at Theudas's mid-section. In one quick move, Theudas grabbed Malachi by the arms and effortlessly flung him to the ground.

"How many times must I tell you?" Theudas panted. "You must plan your attack, anticipate your opponent's moves. If you do not, then I fear you will always be on your back in battle."

Shaking his head, Malachi stood up. "Father, I do not understand. Why do you push me so hard? I have plenty of time to learn."

"Son, none of us knows how much time the Lord will give us on this Earth!" Theudas snapped. "Now, get into position."

With the noonday sun beating down on his back,

Malachi once again took a crouching stance. Digging his sandaled feet into the rocky ground, he again lunged at Theudas. This time the old man grabbed Malachi by the leg, then using his shoulder, forced the boy to the ground.

Theudas shook his head. "Son, you are not in combat with the Earth." He chuckled to himself as he turned his back to Malachi and looked out over the side of the cliff where they practiced. "Get off the ground and focus!"

Malachi felt a twinge of anger building in his gut. Leaping to his feet, he rushed the old man from behind. As he wrapped his arms around Theudas, the old man instinctively stepped forward, threw the boy over his shoulder and down the side of the mountain.

"Malachi!" Theudas yelled, rushing to the edge. Looking down, he was horrified to see the boy bounce several yards before coming to a stop on a ledge. "Do not try to move, son, I am coming down."

Theudas began a frantic descent down the side of the steep, rocky mountain. When he reached Malachi, Theudas was stunned. The boy was completely unharmed.

"How can this be?" Theudas said, frantically inspecting Malachi up and down. "You are not even scratched!" Theudas dropped to his knees and rejoiced. "God be praised! It is another miracle!"

"What do you mean, Father, another miracle?" asked Malachi.

"My son, let us return home," Theudas said, excitedly, pulling Malachi to his feet. "It is time we discussed, like men, the nature of your existence."

Malachi and Theudas began the slow climb back up the mountain. When the two had reached the caves they called home, Theudas motioned for Malachi to sit down with him at the fire.

"I remember the day I took you away from the tribe," Theudas recalled, staring into the embers. "You were just nine days old. The tribe would not have been happy, had I not brought you here."

Malachi's eyes grew wide. "What do you mean, Father."

Theudas stroked the fire with a stick. "You see, my son, you were born of a human mother, but she had not yet been with any man. We put her through a Bisha'a, and the Lord's judgment was in her favor." Theudas paused, then looked solemnly into Malachi's face. "No man came forward to claim you as his son. You are to my knowledge, only half mortal."

Malachi stood up. "So, you are not my blood father?"

"No, not by blood," Theudas said, "but I took you, because no one else would. That makes you my son."

Malachi took a step back. "But you said another miracle. What others have there been?"

"Malachi," the old man said, rising, "I have tried to make light of the fact that you almost never eat, or that you can go days without any need for sleep. It was foolish not to tell you. I had hoped all these things were just the imaginings of a silly old man. But, then, today, you fall down the side of a mountain, but suffered no injuries. I can no longer deny it, your birth was divinely inspired."

Malachi suddenly dropped to his knees in front of Theudas, sobbing. "Father, I beg you, forgive me!" Malachi cried. "I attacked you in anger."

The old man placed his hand on the boy's head. "It is

I that need you to forgive me," Theudas said. "I should have told you these things from the beginning, not waited until you were a man of eighteen."

Theudas took Malachi by the hands and helped him to his feet. With a loving touch, he smoothed the boy's hair then gave him a strong pat on the back.

"I do not know what the Lord has planned for you, my son," Theudas said, "so we will continue to keep a watchful eye and listen for His voice. Now, I am off for some firewood."

The old man turned to leave.

"Wait!" Malachi called out.

"Son, practice your moves," Theudas said over his shoulder, "I will not be long."

Malachi shook his head as he watched the only father he had ever known disappear from view. He returned to the fire and tossed in a few more sticks. Malachi stared into the flames for several minutes, letting all that Theudas had told him sink in. Half human? He rubbed his eyes and tried to imagine what the his real father was like. Who was he? Angel? Demon? But his concentration was suddenly interrupted by the sounds of men shouting.

"Father?" Malachi said to himself.

Breaking into a run, he made his way down the trail. The voices grew louder as Malachi got closer to the trade road that passed through the area. Cautiously, he peered over a pair of large sun-bleached rocks. There he saw Theudas, lying on the ground while a small squadron of Egyptian soldiers beat him. One by one, each man took his turn, kicking the old man. The sounds of Theudas's bones cracking, echoed up through the pass.

Enraged, Malachi leapt over the rocks and confronted them. "Leave him be, Egyptian pigs!"

Grabbing at the soldiers, Malachi shoved them away. The men stepped back and formed a circle around the boy and his father. Then one of the Egyptians, dressed more grandly than the others, stepped forward.

"*Filthy sand dweller,*" he sneered, looking Malachi up and down. "You dare to put your hands on the pharaoh's soldiers?" The Egyptian pulled his sword from its sheath and pressed it against Malachi's throat. "I could kill you. I *should* kill you. Give me a reason to spare your worthless hide."

The rest of the squadron laughed as their leader circled Malachi and Theudas. Stopping behind him, the soldier kicked Malachi hard in the small of his back.

"I asked you a question!" he snarled.

"Please," Malachi begged, picking himself up off of the ground, "my father is old. Have mercy for his sake."

The soldier smiled. "There, was that so hard?"

The Egyptian sheathed his sword and returned to the rest of his squadron.

"You sand dwellers are a plague on this land," he said. "Tell your father, the next time he seeks wood for his fire, to be sure he is not in my path."

Chuckling, the Egyptians mounted their horses and rode off. Malachi turned to his father, hoping to see Theudas on his feet. His heart sank instantly. Lying on the ground, the old man was badly bruised, his face bloody and torn.

"Father!" Malachi cried, rushing to Theudas's side. "Can you stand?"

Theudas coughed hard, sending a mist of blood into the air. "No, my son, my legs are broken."

Malachi looked down at the old man's legs and winced. Bones had pushed their way through the skin on Theudas's shins. Anger began to swell in the pit of Malachi's stomach. As the fury intensified, he could sense another presence entering his mind. As the foreign entity pressed deeper into Malachi's head, flashes of violent images began to appear. He could see himself and the Egyptian soldier locked in combat. With clenched fists, he pounded the soldier's face, flattening his nose and blackening his kohl rimmed eyes. Then suddenly, Malachi saw himself rip the soldier's still beating heart from his bloody chest.

"Malachi!" a voice echoed.

Snapping back from his vision, Malachi looked into the eyes of his father.

"My son," Theudas whispered, "your eyes, your— face—I—you—"

Malachi cradled the old man in his arms. "Do not try to speak, Father. You must save your strength."

Theudas pushed Malachi away. "My God, Tobias was right," he whispered slowly, "your father truly was a demon, I see that now."

"Father, no," Malachi said.

"I did not want to believe it." Theudas coughed. "I did not want to believe you were a child of Hell."

Malachi shook his head, fighting back tears. "No, I am *your* son!"

"Malachi, I am going to die here," Theudas said. "Listen to me. There is still hope. You must live a righteous life. You may have come from darkness, but the Lord surely would have struck you dead like the children of the fallen, if He did not have a plan. You were meant for something great. This is my blessing for you."

"What do I do?" Malachi asked.

"As I have always said, listen for His voice," Theudas whispered. "He will redeem you, just like your mother."

Tears streamed down Malachi's face. "I will do as you ask, Father," he said, "I swear to you."

"I know you want revenge," Theudas said in a fading voice, "but you must be patient. Vengeance belongs to the Lord, and no one else."

Theudas closed his eyes and let out a heavy sigh.

"Father?" Malachi cried. He pressed his ear to the old man's chest, but heard nothing. His father was gone, and Malachi was alone.

CHAPTER 8

Beams of blue light streaked across the floor of the hundred-year-old vestry. A gift to St. Bartholomew's Anglican Church in 1959, the stained glass windows had been casting a peaceful glow on the priest's dressing room for nearly sixty years. The soft blue hue, combined with the richness of the dark wood walls, created a tranquil environment for prayer.

"Damn it! Where'd that woman put my stole?" Caleb grumbled to himself. "I've got to stop letting an old lady do my laundry."

Father Caleb rifled through a few more drawers, growing more frustrated. Services started in twenty minutes, and he wasn't even dressed.

"I think I'm going kill her!" he shouted. Defeated, Caleb flopped down into a small wooden chair.

"Father Glass!" a high-pitched, creaky voice scolded, "I spent two hours ironing those vestments! And now your behind is getting them all wrinkled."

Caleb looked up and saw a very angry Pearl Watersen standing in the door way. He lifted a cheek and pulled his now wrinkled green stole out from under his rump.

"Oh! Pearl." Caleb blushed, standing up quickly. "I didn't hear you come in. Is there something I can do for you?"

"I was just on my way to the chapel and thought I would stop in and say hello," she said, raising a disapproving eyebrow. "I guess it's a good thing I did."

Caleb had to admit Pearl was always there to save him from small disasters. It never failed, if Caleb lost it, broke it, or sat on it, eighty-seven-year-old four-foot-eleven Pearl Watersen would make things right. He smiled to himself as he hoisted the now crumpled stole over his head.

"Yep, I don't know what I'd do without you, Pearl," he said. "You've been a huge help to me these last couple of years."

Pearl's face beamed with pride. "Why, Father Glass, that is such a sweet thing to say! Since my Harvey passed on, my hands have felt so idle. But having you here to look after has been such a blessing for me!" Pearl reached up and patted Caleb on the cheek. "Have I told you about my Harvey?"

Rolling his eyes, Caleb sat back down to put on his shoes. *Only about twenty times a week for the past two and half years.*

Pearl rambled on for another five minutes about Harvey's rose bushes while Caleb finished getting ready.

"…but Harvey always swore by garlic juice to get rid of aphids."

Finally Caleb bent down and took Pearl by the shoulders. "Pearl, I need to spend some time with the Lord before services start," he said quietly. "I'll see you later, okay?"

"Of course you do, Father Glass," the old woman said, with a wink. "Put in a good word for me."

Caleb blew out a long sigh as Pearl left the vestry. He

walked over to a large oval mirror hanging on the wall and stared at his own tired face. A heavy, but familiar ache settled on his heart.

"Ten minutes till show time," Caleb said to himself. "Think you can handle it?"

The image in the mirror began to shift, as if he were looking into a funhouse mirror. Caleb looked away for a moment, his eyes burning from trying to focus. When he looked back, his image was clear again, but something seemed wrong. His face was different somehow, angry and dark. Caleb pressed his fingers into his cheeks. He leaned forward, his nose inches from the mirror, trying to examine his now sinister face. Then his image in the mirror began to speak on its own.

"I don't know, can you?" it said, sarcastically. "You're the idiot who wanted to be a priest!"

Startled, Caleb fell backward, crashing into a small cabinet. He stood there for a moment, staring at the mirror, his mouth agape.

"Caleb," it called out, "get your sorry ass over here, I'm not done talking to you!"

Trembling, Caleb slowly crossed himself, then walked back over and stood in front of the mirror, clutching his Pectoral cross. The image smiled at him with a menacing grin.

"You're so pathetic," the image spat. "Every damn week it's the same old crap! You stand here and you whine to me about how much you can't handle this job, how you're sorry you became a priest—Blah, Blah, Blah! I'm ready to puke!"

"But, you don't understand," Caleb began.

"Oh, I understand!" the image yelled back. "I was there too, remember? I was there to bear witness to you running away like the coward you are!"

Tears began to well up in Caleb's eyes. It had been eleven years since John and Madeline Glass had died. The images of their dead bodies at the wake were as fresh in Caleb's mind as if it had happened yesterday. The pictures in the paper had been horrible. Caleb could still see the twisted metal and shattered windows that had been the family mini-van.

Caleb was fourteen when his parents died. He remembered listening to the priest at the funeral remind the tear-streaked crowd that John and Maddie were in a better place. That day Caleb watched the old priest and was amazed. No tears. No pain. The old guy didn't look as if anything could shake him. After the service, Caleb asked the priest if funerals made him sad.

"Of course not, my boy," the priest had replied, "we're at war with the devil! Your parents have joined up with the greatest army there is. The Lord is with them, young Caleb, don't you worry. And although you may miss them, you should rejoice. After all, they have gone home to be with Jesus."

Caleb wanted to feel peace. As soon as he could, he went into seminary, burying himself and his sorrows in the church. A bead of clear snot ran from his nose. Shaking off the memory, Caleb wiped his face.

"Pfft! Mom and Dad would be so proud," the image scoffed, shaking its head. "The Very Reverend Broken Glass can't get through a Sunday without crying like a little bitch! Why don't you just quit?"

"Shut up!" Caleb yelled back at the mirror. "You listen to me—" he started. But the dark image of Caleb was gone. Furious, he banged on the mirror with both fists, the glass spider-webbing where he punched it. "You come back here!" he screamed.

At that moment, the organist began to belt out the opening hymn. Startled, Caleb opened his eyes and looked around. He found himself still sitting in the wooden chair. Curiously, he reached down, and pulled the green stole out from under his behind.

"What the hell?" Caleb said, holding the stole up. He shook his head, as he put the stole on. Then, cautiously, Caleb stood and walked over to the mirror. He gazed into it, smiling weakly. "What a horrible dream."

He knew he was fooling himself. Dream or no, the mirror knew the truth. Today would be as painful as all of the other Sundays, and as usual, Caleb would face it alone.

A low sigh echoed from the vestry wall mirror. The dark image of Caleb reappeared for just a moment. A menacing smile spread across its face, as the mirror began to warp and distort. When the image cleared, the face was no longer Father Caleb Glass, but of Lucifer. In an instant, Lucifer's arm shot out through the glass, his strong clawed hand grabbing Caleb by the throat.

"That was no dream," Lucifer growled.

Caleb twisted and pulled, trying to release himself from the dark lord's grip. But, the more he struggled, the weaker he seemed to become. Caleb could feel a hotness behind his eyes as he began to pass out. Just as the blackness was about to take him, Caleb could feel his breathing return. Slowly, his eyes focused. The mirror once again, was back to normal.

Caleb dropped to his knees, gasping. He turned over the back side of one end of his stole, and wiped his face.

"Why does this keep happening?" he said. "Am I going crazy?"

But the room was once again calm and silent. Caleb stood back up, straightened his vestments, then headed toward the door.

With a heavy heart, and a mind full of questions, Caleb took one last glance around the room then left the vestry to start Sunday services.

CHAPTER 9

609 B.C., Tel Megiddo

As dawn rose up from the east, Malachi stood high on his mountain, listening to the war drums. The squabbling between Egypt and Judah had been growing for some time. Malachi had learned from travelers on the trade routes that King Josiah planned to face the Pharaoh Neco and settle their differences, once and for all.

"Egyptian pigs," Malachi muttered. "Sixteen hundred years and yet so many things have not changed."

Grabbing his bed roll and walking stick, Malachi began his descent down the mountain. He had decided a few days before, that the war was the sign he had been looking for. Malachi knew he couldn't face Neco's army alone, but the Lord favored King Josiah, so Malachi decided to seek an audience with the ruler of Judah.

It took Malachi two weeks to reach the holy city of Jerusalem. As he entered the gates, he was awestruck by the massive stone walls and the smells of animals and food blending with incense and olive blossoms. The city was bustling with street vendors, selling everything from bread and wine, to idols and rebellion.

When he finally reached the king's palace, Malachi was

greeted by a pair of Judean guards.

"I am Malachi Ben Sinai," he said to the guards, "and I have come to seek an audience with King Josiah."

The guard to his left stepped forward. Reaching out, the guard took Malachi's bed roll and turned it out on the ground. While he was searching Malachi's things, the other guard patted him down. Satisfied that he carried no weapons, the two guards stepped back.

"Understand that we must search you before you enter the house of the king," the first guard said. "What is your business here?"

Malachi gathered his bedroll in his arms. "I have heard the war drums of the Egyptians," he said, "and have come to pledge myself and my loyalty to Judah."

"And you wish to tell the king that you want to fight in his army?" the guard asked.

Malachi bowed deeply. "I will kill many Egyptians for him, yes."

The two guards looked at each other then began to burst with laughter. The first guard turned back to Malachi and waved him away.

"You are no soldier," he said, wiping a tear from his eye. "King Josiah requires his army to be made of seasoned warriors, not boys who live in caves."

Angry, Malachi threw his things back on the ground and took a crouched position. "Come at me with all you have," he said, "and I will show you I am more than just a boy who lives in caves."

The guard raised an eyebrow at the challenge.

"Show the whelp what Judah's army can do," the other guard said, clapping him on the back.

"Very well, Malachi Ben Sinai," the guard said, taking a wide stance, "if you can best me, I will make sure you see the king."

For a few moments, both Malachi and his opponent silently stalked each other, circling like vultures above a carcass.

A voice in Malachi's head suddenly pushed its way in from the past. "You must plan your attack," the voice echoed, "anticipate your opponent's moves."

Malachi quickly studied the body language of the guard. He was standing too high, as if he wanted Malachi to attack him low. In that moment, he knew just what to do.

"Well, come on whelp," the guard said, "make a move."

Malachi burst forward, grabbing for the guard's right leg. The guard wrapped his arms around Malachi's waist, as if to pick him up, but Malachi was faster. He pulled the guard's leg out from under him, dropping the man down flat on his back. Before the guard could catch his breath, Malachi slammed a knee down hard on the guard's chest.

Smiling, Malachi leaned down close to the guard's face. "Do you wish to continue?" he asked.

"No," the guard said, coughing, "you have made your point."

Malachi stood up and helped the man to his feet. He then took a few steps back and waited for the guard to speak. He didn't have to wait long.

"I am impressed, Malachi Ben Sinai," the guard said, dusting himself off. "You had an excellent teacher. My name is Jahdai."

"My father, Theudas, was killed many years ago by soldiers of Egypt," Malachi said solemnly. "I have been patient in my quest for vengeance up until now. Will you take me to the king?"

Jahdai nodded. "I am a man of my word. Follow me."

Together, Jahdai and Malachi entered the house of the king. They walked for several minutes, trekking through long corridors until finally reaching the main throne room of King Josiah.

Jahdai motioned for Malachi to stay at the door. Then Jahdai walked to the foot of the throne, dropped to one knee, and bowed his head. "My King," he said, staring at the floor, "a young man from the mountains of Sinai wishes to speak with you. He has come to pledge his life and loyalty to Judah."

King Josiah leaned forward in his throne to get a better look at Malachi. Saying nothing, Josiah waved Malachi forward. Whispers from the king's court surrounded Malachi like a fog, as he walked toward the throne. He came to a stop next to Jahdai then dropped to a knee beside him.

"Rise, stranger, so I can see your face more clearly," Josiah said. His voice was strong and full of authority, yet surprisingly gentle.

Malachi stood and looked directly into the face of the King of Judah.

"So," the king said, "you have come to pledge yourself to Judah. Tell me, what do you bring to my kingdom that Yahweh does not already provide?"

"Good king, would you do me the honor of allowing me to speak to you in private?" Malachi asked. "What I have to say is of a sensitive nature."

Josiah thought for a moment then nodded. He clapped his hands twice, signaling to the people in his court to leave the room. As courtiers, servants, and guards filed out of the room, Jahdai turned to Malachi and winked.

"It is a good sign, my friend," he said in a low voice, "if the king is willing to see you alone. Good luck to you. I look forward to fighting at your side on the battlefield."

With that, Jahdai left the throne room as well, leaving Malachi alone with King Josiah.

"Well, boy, you have my attention." the king said, "What is it you wish to say that cannot be said in front of my court?"

Malachi shifted nervously where he stood. An instant feeling of doubt crept in. He wondered if the king would believe him and worried about what would happen if he didn't.

"Good king," Malachi began, "you and I have a common enemy in Egypt. My father was murdered by Egyptians—" He paused, thinking back to that horrible day.

"Yes, go on," Josiah prompted.

Malachi took a deep breath. "—almost two millennia ago."

Josiah sat silent for a few moments, pondering what was just said. Then, without any expression, said, "Continue."

"He was not my blood father, you see," said Malachi. "He was just the man who raised me. It is believed that my true father is a—demon." Malachi held his breath. He had never uttered those words aloud before. He studied Josiah's face as he let those words sink in. Again, Josiah wore no expression.

The king stood up and stretched. "Is that so?" he said, sternly. "What does the unfortunate circumstance of your birth have to do with my kingdom?"

"My father, Theudas, believed that the Lord had a purpose for my existence. He told me with his dying breath to listen for the Lord's voice. Then I heard the war drums of Pharaoh Neco's army. The time to avenge my father is now, and I believe by serving a righteous king, I will be redeemed by God."

"I see," Josiah said as he sat back down. "I hope you understand, that if what you say is true, serving in my army will not guarantee your redemption," he said calmly. "It is just as likely that pharaoh's drums have called you to face God's wrath. Do you accept that reality?"

Malachi nodded his head. "Yes, I do."

"Know this, Malachi Ben Sinai," the king warned, "I serve the One True God. I have toiled long and hard to eliminate false gods from my kingdom. If I even suspect that you are in league with the devil, I will surely kill you myself. Do we have an understanding?"

"Yes," Malachi said, "we have an understanding."

"Have you told anyone else this story?" Josiah asked.

Malachi shook his head. "No, your Majesty, I do not wish to scare people, only to be free of the chains of my father's curse."

"You are a wise boy, Malachi Ben Sinai," Josiah said, "I will be praying for you."

"And I am indebted to you for trusting me," Malachi

replied.

"Very well, my strange friend," Josiah said, "go and see Jahdai. He will set you up with lodgings."

Malachi bowed. "Thank you, your Majesty." Then he turned on his heel and exited the throne room. As he walked out into the hall, a small voice whispered to him from behind a large stone pillar.

"You there, stranger!"

He turned and saw a beautiful servant girl step out from behind it. She tossed her head back, swishing a thick black mane of hair over her shoulder. The young woman's hips sashayed seductively as she approached him, while a strand of tiny bells played a haunting melody from around her ankle.

"I am Zilpah, a servant to the king," she said slowly, fluttering her long eyelashes. "I was listening to what you said in there. If you ask me, I think you are going to pass on a golden opportunity."

Malachi frowned. "What do you mean?"

Zilpah draped her arms around his neck and leaned in close. Malachi could smell perfumed oil on her cool skin. The scent was musky and thick. A twinge of arousal prickled the back of his neck, as he breathed in her sexy scent. His hands instinctively came up, clutching her small waist. The glint in her eye was as intoxicating as her smell.

"The prophets have told Josiah that Judah will fall," she whispered, gently chewing on his earlobe. "Then, as if sent by Ba'al himself, you appear. That fool king believes his One True God will prevail, but how can that be, when his own prophets say otherwise?" Zilpah pressed herself against Malachi's chest. "I believe it is you that will prevail. Kill Josiah, and take your place as the new King of Judah!"

Her words cut through Malachi's lust-driven haze. He took a hold of her arms and peeled the servant girl off his neck. Then he stepped back from her and shook his head. "You are mistaken, servant," he said coldly. "I have no desire to be a murderer or a king. My only wish is to be a man."

"But you heard what Josiah said," Zilpah said, growing angry. "What if serving him gets you nothing? Serve Ba'al, and you shall have everything you desire." Again, Zilpah tried to embrace Malachi. "Take me," she moaned, "make me what you are, and I will stand beside you, as your queen! Ba'al will make you ruler of all the world!"

Malachi grabbed Zilpah again and shoved her to the ground. Zilpah landed hard, splitting her forehead on the stone floor. Blood began to ooze from the wound, crawling down her face like tears. Without a word, Malachi turned and walked away.

"You will be sorry, demon!" Zilpah yelled at his back. "Judah will bleed, and Ba'al will see you in *Hell*!"

CHAPTER 10

Pharaoh Neco's army filtered into the Jezreel Valley with the westward winds. It had been over a month since he and his forces had departed from Carchemish. The trip had been a quiet and somewhat peaceful one. But the time for pleasantry ended when they arrived in the land of Judah.

At the eastern end of Tel Megiddo stood King Josiah's army and a battle Neco didn't have time for. The pharaoh sighed heavily as he gazed across the valley into thousands of faces, blindly ready for war. His fight wasn't with the Judeans. Neco's only desire was to defeat the Babylonians, and expand the empire. But King Josiah wouldn't listen.

An Egyptian soldier on horseback parted Josiah's army and made his way across the valley floor. When the soldier reached the pharaoh's chariot, he dismounted and bowed to his king.

"What news from our Judean neighbors?" asked Neco. "Has he changed his mind? Will he let us pass through his lands, or no?"

The soldier shook his head, still staring at the ground. "No, my lord, King Josiah says we cannot pass. Shall I return with your response?"

Neco wiped his face with his hands then looked behind him at his men. Tens of thousands of foot soldiers, mercenaries, and archers along with a five-thousand-horse cavalry and two hundred chariots stared back at him, waiting.

"No," he said, turning back to the soldier, "return to your place on the line. I will deliver the message myself."

Neco snapped the reins and turned his horse and chariot around to face his men. But before he could open his mouth to speak, a delicate hand brushed his shoulder.

"Great Pharaoh, it is time you presented the Sun God to the troops. Knowing that their god is with them in battle, will surly raise their spirits."

The pharaoh closed his eyes in disgust. He could feel his blood boil with contempt at the sound of Lilith's voice. A constant irritant, Lilith had not given Neco a moment's peace since he took the throne. Many leaders before him had tried to dispose of her, but none had succeeded. Lilith had the protection of the Sun God, Ra.

"Yes, my lady," Neco said over his shoulder, "I suppose it would."

As if on cue, a lone rider in Egyptian armor approached the pharaoh's chariot. The rider pulled his horse up alongside the chariot then leaned over and kissed Lilith gently on the cheek.

"Greetings, Mother," he said.

"Ra, my beautiful son." Lilith beamed. "Are you ready to fulfill your destiny?"

Ra nodded, a wicked smile creeping across his handsome face. "Are you certain he will be here?"

"Oh yes," she answered, "the priests have seen it in the signs. Azazael's son is among the Jews. Here, I have something for you."

Lilith reached into the folds of her wraps and pulled out a golden dagger. She lovingly gazed at it for a moment, admiring its hard lines and jewel-studded hilt, then handed it to Ra.

"The high priest himself covered this dagger with spells from the Book of the Dead. I call it The Soul Stealer. It is a far more dangerous weapon than any sword wielded by mortal men. It does not just kill a man, it also takes his soul. The strength of the man absorbs into the blade. The more you kill, the stronger the weapon and my gift to you."

Ra turned the dagger over in his hands. Indeed, the weapon was covered from end to end with hieroglyphics. The gleam on its blade reflected in his eyes with the fury of a star. A fitting weapon for the self-proclaimed god of the sun. Ra shoved the knife into his waistband and dismounted. Then, he turned his attention to the pharaoh.

"I think it would be best for me to place myself on the ground with the rest of the army," he said. "I want to be close to the people I intend to rule."

Neco said nothing.

"You would be wise to acknowledge my son in front of the men, Neco," Lilith hissed. "There should be no confusion about who is the true ruler of Egypt."

Neco turned and glared at her defiantly. "There is no confusion, my lady."

Raising his staff in the air, Neco called out to his legions. "Soldiers of Egypt," he began, "the King of Judah has chosen to deny us passage through the Jezreel Valley. Though we seek to defeat a common enemy, Josiah has chosen to stand in our way. But our determination to crush Babylon under our feet will not be swayed!" Neco paused, as the soldiers erupted in cheers. He glanced over at Ra and was met with a smug smile. Swallowing hard, the pharaoh continued. "The gods have blessed us with a mighty warrior. To ensure we are victorious, Ra, God of the Sun, has come down from the heavens and chosen to stand beside you in this battle!"

Neco motioned to Ra to step forward. With his fists held high in the air, Ra proudly faced the finest warriors in all of Egypt. "I promise you," Ra called out, "the Jews will be defeated this day, and afterward, I shall hand you the sons and daughters of Babylon!"

The cheers from pharaoh's army grew as Lilith stepped down from the chariot. Then she mounted Ra's horse and trotted over to her beloved son.

"Make me proud of you," she said, reaching down and stroking Ra's hair. "Find the half breed and kill him. It is your destiny."

Ra bowed to his mother then slapped the back end of the horse as she rode off.

Neco positioned his chariot front and center. He could see the Judean forces were lined up and waiting for him to make the first move. With the wind at his back, Neco raised his staff again and gave the signal.

Both Judean and Egyptian forces broke into a full run, meeting in the center of the valley. As swords and shields clashed, hundreds of arrows streaked the sky, raining death down onto the battle below. Thunder from thousands of hooves cut through the air as pharaoh's cavalry barreled down on King Josiah's army, while the rumble of chariots echoed like monsters spat out from

Hades.

With his dagger in hand, Ra cut down Josiah's men, one after another, each one losing their soul at the thrust of his blade. He cleared a path into the center of the fighting, his rage focused on finding the half breed. As far back as Ra could remember, his mother could speak of nothing else but the death of the great Azazael's son.

In the midst of the chaos, a man caught his attention. He was young, but fought with the ferocity and skill of a seasoned warrior. For a moment, all Ra could do was watch in wonder, as the young man savagely cut down every Egyptian soldier he came across. Then he turned, and set his sights on Ra.

Breaking into a sprint, the Judean was in Ra's face within seconds. Using his shield, he landed a blow to the Sun God, snapping his head back. Unharmed, Ra fought back with a punch to the kidneys. Back and forth, the two exchanged blows with no results.

"You are him, are you not?" Ra finally asked, panting.

The Judean stepped back. "Who?" he asked.

"The son of Azazael," Ra answered, "The demon half breed. You must be him, for no mortal man on this Earth could match me blow for blow."

"My name is Malachi Ben Sinai," the Judean said. "How is it that you know of my birth?"

"It does not matter, Malachi Ben Sinai," Ra growled, twirling the dagger in his hand. "It is my destiny to kill you. That is all you need to know."

Ra lunged at Malachi with the dagger. Malachi grabbed Ra's arm and threw him to the ground. Jumping to his feet, Ra prepared for another attack, when the deafening sound of silence pierced his ears.

Through the dust and smoke, he saw Pharaoh Neco standing over the King of Judah. Josiah, defeated and bleeding, had just enough strength to get to his knees. Then with one thrust, Neco ran his staff through King Josiah's chest. Its sharpened point bursting through his back, pinning him to the ground.

With their king dead, the Judeans were defeated. By the hundreds, what was left of Josiah's army began to flee. As the battle disintegrated around him, Ra turned his attention back to Malachi.

"It is your turn to die, half breed!" he snarled.

Ra tackled Malachi, pinning him to the ground. He pressed the blade of his dagger to Malachi's throat.

"But before I kill you and steal your soul," Ra whispered, "I want to see it. Show me your demon."

An ancient rage began to swell in Malachi's belly. He had not felt its presence since the day Theudas had died. Images of Ra began to flash in his mind. Malachi could see himself, holding Ra by the throat with one hand then, with a flick of his wrist, snapping his neck like a twig.

Ra watched half smiling, as Malachi began to transform. His eyes, normally a clear chestnut brown, glowed a fiery red. Malachi twisted and growled, as his cheekbones began to push out from under his skin, and his teeth, now more like fangs, sharpened themselves to fine points.

Lilith approached them from behind. She was anxious to witness Azazael's bastard child die. But her heart nearly burst from her chest when she saw Malachi.

"Finish him!" she screamed. "He has his father's

power! You cannot let him complete the transformation, finish it *now!*"

Ra raised The Soul Stealer above his head with both hands. Taking a deep breath, he tried to bring the dagger down, but suddenly a gust of wind ripped the weapon from Ra's grasp.

"*No!*" Lilith screamed, dropping to her knees.

Swirling clouds of black sulfurous smoke rose up from the ground. Within seconds, the smoke blocked out the setting sun. A red glowing light pierced the darkness, growing larger, then splitting into two forms—Lucifer and Azazael.

Lucifer strolled around Ra and Malachi, glancing at the two of them with his black eyes. He reached down and touched Malachi's forehead. A wave of calm washed over him, as the demon within him began to fade. Lucifer watched as Malachi returned to normal, the dark lord's face filled with fascination and curiosity.

"Lord Lucifer," Lilith stuttered, "spare me, please. I meant no disrespect—"

Instantly, Lucifer's hand shot out and slapped her face. The impact sent a stream of blood from her nose to the ground. Lucifer, still silent, glanced over at Ra. Without a word, he snatched the Sun God up by the neck and flung him to the ground beside Malachi. Azazael smiled triumphantly as he stepped over Ra and took his place beside Lucifer.

"As you can see, everything is just as I said it would be, brother," Azazael said with a smirk.

Lucifer pulled The Soul Stealer from his cloak. He closed his eyes for a moment and licked the edge of the blade seductively. Then he opened his eyes and fixed his gaze on Lilith's bloody face.

"Yes, brother," Lucifer said evenly, "she is a typical, predictable human."

Chapter 11

"When you did not return to our happy home," Lucifer began. "I realized that Azazael knew you much better than I did." He paused, absently picking his long fingernails with Ra's dagger. "Did you actually think that because you were not in Hell, I would not know where you were?"

"Mercy," Lilith groaned, "I beg you."

The dark lord turned his back to her and smiled at Azazael. "I will give you what you deserve."

Whipping back around, Lucifer took hold of Lilith's long black hair. Her hands shot up, trying in vain to loosen Lucifer's iron grip. He glanced over at Azazael then extended his arm, offering Lilith to him.

"I believe this belongs to you, brother," Lucifer said.

Azazael reached over and grabbed Lilith by the arm. He pressed her to his chest and whispered in her ear. "When I return to Hell," he hissed, "I am going to break you, my precious toy." Azazael chuckled, pulling the charred black box from his cloak with his free hand. "Remember this? Very soon it will be your soul's new home. Trapped inside the dry bones of my wife for all eternity."

With both hands, Azazael grasped Lilith's shoulders and spun her around to face Lucifer. His eyes met the dark lord's with a knowing expression. Then nodding to his master, Azazael released his grip on Lilith and stepped back.

"No, please!" she begged.

Ignoring her pleas, Lucifer snapped his fingers. The ground under Lilith began to rumble and shake. Dozens of rotted human arms shot up out of the ground, grabbing hold of Lilith's legs. Within seconds, the mother of the Sun God was once again banished to Hell.

Malachi watched the scene with shock and fear. He wondered what the devil would do with him—and if he was strong enough to resist.

"Stand up, my son, and speak not a word," a voice whispered in his ear. "Do nothing to provoke the wrath of Lord Lucifer."

Malachi looked up and found himself staring into the face of Azazael. Obediently, Malachi rose from the ground and dusted himself off. Azazael wrapped a protective arm around Malachi, then put a finger to his lips and winked at him.

Lucifer turned his attention to Ra. "And what do we have here?" he said sardonically, pointing the dagger at Ra. "There is only one who has the right to call himself a god, and you are not he! Come here, boy."

Ra stood up and walked toward Lucifer. His mind raced, searching for a way to survive this situation. Not wanting to suffer the same punishment as his mother, Ra bowed deeply.

"My lord, Lucifer, it would be my pleasure to serve you."

"Yes, it would." Lucifer sneered. "Do not fret, serve

me you shall indeed. But this time, my servant will be on a much shorter leash."

Lucifer raised his hand to the sky, casting a long shadow across Ra's face from the moonlight. "You will not live as freely among the humans as your treacherous mother did," he said. "The Sun God you will be no more," Lucifer called out. "From this night on, the sun is your eternal enemy. Its mighty power will burn your flesh to dust. You will live in the shadows of night, or perish."

Ra's face fell. How he loved to bask in the morning sun. Ripples of anger tore through him. Thinking of his mother's fate, Ra quickly squashed those feelings.

"And since you are so fond of being worshiped by humans, I will take that away as well." Lucifer dropped his hand back down to his side. At that moment, a terrible hunger roared in Ra's stomach, then spread through his veins like fire. Ra doubled over, trying not to vomit.

"Ah," Lucifer said, flashing a fanged grin, "the hunger has erupted inside your stinking guts. You will thirst for the blood of humans, for all time, boy. The life-giving fluid that flows through them will haunt your dreams like ghosts. You will need it to live, and those who used to praise your name will now shrink from you in fear."

Lucifer turned and began to walk back into the swirling wall of smoke. Without looking back, he called out to Azazael, "Are you coming, brother?"

Azazael shook his head. "I have some business to finish here. But I will see you soon."

As the dark prince faded into the sulfur, Azazael heard Lucifer laugh. Azazael looked down at Malachi, a loving expression peeking out from behind his eyes. The demon could see that the humans he hated so much had raised his son well.

"I feel I owe you an explanation," Azazael began.

Malachi held up his hand in protest. "Stop, you do not owe me anything. My life has been a blessing from Yahweh. I will do what I need to do in order to fulfill His plan for me."

Azazael winced at hearing the name of the Most High. The purity of His name burned his ears like the flames of Hell itself.

"So," Azazael replied, "you desire the things that are Above?"

"I wish to be embraced by the Lord," Malachi answered, "and be welcomed into the Kingdom of Heaven."

Azazael pondered what his son was telling him. Secretly, he too sometimes wished he could undo his own sins. Azazael knew it was too late for him, but there was a way to save Malachi from eternal damnation.

"Hold out your arm, my son," he said abruptly.

Malachi gave the demon a nervous look. Then without a word, he pulled up the sleeve of his tunic, exposing the muscular flesh of his right arm. Azazael reached out and grasped Malachi's forearm. A searing pain rang out from his skin. After a moment, Azazael pulled his hand away, exposing a strange wound.

"What is this?" Malachi panted, inspecting his arm. The surface of his now swollen arm was covered with strange writing. "What have you done to me?"

"Son," Azazael said. "As the ages pass, I grow more and more evil in nature. But there is just enough of the

Above still in me, to give you this one gift."

Malachi was intrigued. "What does it say?"

"It is forbidden for me to speak the words," Azazael answered. "All I can tell you is that it is sacred text, written in the most ancient of languages. You must stop looking for *signs* from the Most High—" Azazael swallowed hard, "—and begin to look for the Most High, in the flesh."

"You are both fools!"

Azazael and Malachi turned and stared at Ra.

"My mother warned me about this Most High of yours," he spat. "He is selfish and pigheaded at best! Surely you can see that, can you not, half breed?"

Azazael sighed disgustedly. "I have had my fill of you, child of Lilith!" The demon faced east, then spoke in a strange tongue that Malachi had never heard before. The sun in all its glory began to rise in the night sky. Smoke billowed from Ra, as his flesh began to burn. He ran off into the fumes of Hell, adding his own to the mix. Azazael chuckled and gave Malachi a clap on the back.

"He deserved that."

"Yes," Malachi agreed, "I suppose he did."

Azazael smiled, "I must go now, my son. Know that you are the one good thing I did for the human race."

As he started to walk into the sulfur, Malachi called out to him. "Wait!"

Azazael stopped. "What is it, Malachi?"

"Will I ever see you again?" Malachi asked.

"I once asked The Most High, 'why should I, an angel born of Heaven's fire, revere a creature created from the dust of the ground beneath my feet,'" Azazael answered solemnly. "I have made it my personal business to hate and torment humans. I have spent centuries scheming to steal the souls of men from Heaven's embrace. Believe me when I tell you, you do not want to see me again."

Malachi stared at the ground. He had waited so long, wondering if he would ever meet his real father, fantasizing about what he would say. Now that the moment had come, he was at a loss for words. But it was just as well. When he looked back up, Azazael and all traces of Hell were gone.

CHAPTER 12

The little soul cowered in the corner, its hollow eyes darting back and forth, searching for an escape route. Lucifer took aim, and threw The Soul Stealer, missing the soul, but nailing the wall next to the door.

As he rose from his chair to retrieve the dagger, a knock at the door grabbed his attention.

Lucifer sighed and returned to his seat. "Enter," he called out.

Azazael opened the door and stepped into the room.

"You sent for me, brother?" he asked.

The dark prince motioned for Azazael to sit. It had been over a month since the incident at Tel Meggido, and Azazael had stalled meeting with Lucifer. Azazael knew his master had questions that needed to be answered.

"I have longed to congratulate you, brother, on your victory," Lucifer said. "It must be so satisfying to have avenged your dearly departed wife. Tell me, what have you done with Lilith?"

Azazael shifted in his seat. "She is getting used to her new sleeping arrangements," he replied flashing a devilish grin. "Let us just say, her new chambers are much smaller."

"And no doubt are in the shape of a small black box," Lucifer said, shaking his head.

"Brother, let us be open with each other," Azazael said. "What is the real reason you summoned me here?"

The dark lord stood up and walked across the room. He pulled the dagger out of the wall then returned to his chair. Lucifer remained silent for several minutes, while he sat there twirling the small gold knife. Finally, he spoke. "Do you think it was wise to give your son such a generous gift," he asked. "Information like that is detrimental to our cause. And I could consider that breaking our no contact agreement. Am I justified?"

"On the contrary, brother," Azazael replied. "I waited until after you called the wager. Surely there is no harm in a father giving his only son a present."

Lucifer let Azazael's words hang in the air for a moment. Then he threw his head back and burst into heavy laughter. Soon, they were both laughing, tears evaporating around them.

"Well played, brother, you are a clever one," Lucifer said, taking a deep breath. "So, what is to become of your young man now?"

"I suppose we sit back and see what Malachi does with what he has been given…" the demon answered. Azazael's words trailed off, his eyes gazing out the window of Lucifer's chambers. For a brief moment, he found himself hating his son. The inscription he'd given Malachi was priceless information—information Azazael could never use himself. Mercy was a trophy only mankind could win now. As he listened to the wailings of the damned flowing in through the open window, Azazael could almost feel the walls of jealousy closing in all around him.

Lucifer drew his arm back suddenly and threw the

dagger. This time it hit its target square in the chest, popping the soul like a balloon full of gray fog. The unexpected movement snapped Azazael back from his thoughts.

"Perhaps," Lucifer pondered, his eyes glowing from the excitement of destroying the soul, "you regret your decision?"

It was Azazael's silence that answered his question.

CHAPTER 13

Present Day

Malachi stood quietly, breathing in the sweet fragrances that hung in the morning air. Though the sun had not yet risen, he could tell he was surrounded by roses, honeysuckle, and pine trees.

"I hope the inside of Yahweh's house is as peaceful as His garden," he said to himself.

Through the darkness, Malachi could just make out the outline of St. Bartholomew's Church, and it was obvious that little had changed in over a century. Its beautiful stone archways and heavy oak doors reminded him of so many other houses of worship. The lofty stature of its design let everyone who came in know that this was the dwelling of the almighty God.

As Malachi wandered the chapel grounds, he came to a trail marked *Stations of the Cross*. Casually, he strolled down the dirt path, stopping every so often to admire the detailed stone cuttings that depicted Christ's passion. The lights from the surrounding garden lamps gave the cuttings an eerie, yet comforting, glow.

A change in the wind stopped him in his tracks. The smells in the air shifted, and Malachi realized that he was no longer alone.

"Oh, I remember that day," Ra said calmly, stepping out from behind a large Italian Cyprus and pointing to the stone cutting of Christ on the cross. "It was a pity that you did not make it in time."

Malachi took a deep breath. "How did you find me?" he asked.

Ra put his hand to his chest, feigning hurt feelings. "Is this how you treat all of your friends? No wonder, I am the only one who still comes around."

Malachi stepped forward, his face inches from Ra's. "You are no friend of mine," he snapped, "I asked you a question!"

"Whoa!" Ra exclaimed, putting his hands up. "Relax, half breed, there is no need to get physical. I am only here to talk about what we always talk about."

"You can tell him the same thing I told you to tell him last time," Malachi said, walking away. "Not interested."

"Then you know what I have to do," Ra said in a serious voice.

Malachi stopped and turned around.

"You remember what your stubbornness cost you in Scotland?" Ra paused. "I almost regret that night. You know, I really thought we had finally broken you." He shook his head. "Half breed, you truly are a worthy opponent."

"I am nobody special," Malachi said slowly, "and I have made my decision. Why can he not just leave me alone?"

"Nobody special?" Ra said, his mouth agape, "You are the only son of Hell's greatest general! You have powers that any mortal human would kill for. Why, you should feel duty bound to leave all of this—" Ra waved his hand around. "—and join your real family."

Malachi shook his head. "No, my answer will always be no."

"Then the priest will die, just like the others," Ra said calmly. "Lucifer forbids you to complete the ceremony."

"It is not for him to decide!" Malachi yelled, his patience growing thin. "Show some mercy, Ra, for once in your miserable life. Leave the human alone."

Ra stood motionless for a moment, clicking his tongue and staring off into the night as if in deep thought. "Sorry," he said finally. "Unlike you, I know my place, and I follow orders. So, if you will not come with me to Hell and take your place beside Azazael, I will be forced to kill the priest. Why is this so important to you? Why do you want the love and affection of an invisible taskmaster, who has given you nothing, when Lucifer has offered you the world?"

"Because Lucifer offers merely the world, and for only a moment. Yahweh promises paradise that will last for an eternity," Malachi answered, smiling. "You will never change my mind, Ra. No matter how many priests you kill. You will only succeed in making them martyrs."

Ra shook his head in disgust. "Very well," he said, "the human's blood will flow, and your stubbornness will be to blame, again."

A peachy glow began to brighten the eastern sky. Faint chirping from overhead nests sounded the morning bells.

Ra cringed at the approaching sunlight. "Think about what I said," he whispered, backing into the remaining darkness of a shade tree. "You cannot run forever."

As Ra slipped away, Malachi stood motionless and watched the sunrise. Instinctively, his hand reached up and clutched a large pill shaped pendant hanging around his neck. Ra's words had cut a hole in Malachi's heart. He wished every day that he could take back what had happened on that foggy night, so many years ago.

He brought the pendant to his lips and gently kissed it. "I miss you, my friend," he whispered.

CHAPTER 14

33 A.D., Jerusalem

"I was surprised to see you this year, Malachi," Haran said between bites.

Malachi smiled politely to his guest, while nibbling on a small piece of bread. Haran passed through the badlands of Sinai every year during Passover. It was the only way he and his family could get to Jerusalem. For over thirty years Haran, his wife and children, and now his grandchildren, broke their journey at Malachi's doorstep.

"I thought for sure, that this year you would finally spread your wings and see the world," Haran continued.

"Yes, my friend," Malachi said, chuckling, "but then I would miss your visits. You and your family are nearly the only people I speak to." Malachi bit off another piece of bread. "Would you not miss me?"

Haran frowned. Then he leaned over and whispered something in his wife's ear. Obediently, she quickly got up from her seat near the fire and herded the children to the mouth of the cave, out of earshot.

"I would fear you, if I did not know your heart belongs to Yahweh," Haran said. "I have watched you watch my children grow. I have stood by and kept silent, while you let life pass you by on these dusty old trade routes. Do you think giving me a place to rest one day a year is going to earn you a place in Heaven?"

Malachi shrugged his shoulders. "You are right. I guess I have become complacent," he answered. "But I look forward to seeing you, and I worry about what would happen to you and the family if I were not here."

Haran's mind drifted back thirty years. He had to admit, if Malachi had not rescued him and his wife from bandits all those years ago, his own life would have turned out much differently. He stood up and walked around to where Malachi was sitting. Then he plopped down beside him and took Malachi's hand.

"What are you doing?" Malachi asked, confused.

"I will always be grateful to you, Malachi, for the endless years of hospitality you have shown me and my family," Haran said, looking Malachi in the eyes, "and you will always be a son to me. But, for the sake of your immortal soul, you must go out into the world and find the answers you need. I am happy that you have trusted me with your secret all these years, but if Yahweh had wanted you to just stay here and hide, He would have come down from Heaven and said so."

Haran released Malachi's hand. The two men sat in silence for a few moments.

"You know," Haran said quietly, "there is a man. Some say he is Elijah, others say he is the Messiah. People claim he performs fantastic miracles."

"Is that so?" Malachi asked, leaning in closer. "What kind of miracles?"

"He heals the sick, and he makes the blind see. I have heard that he even raised a man from the dead!" Haran exclaimed.

"Really?" whispered Malachi.

"Yes," Haran whispered back, "which means, it is possible that he can help you. Come with us to Jerusalem, Malachi. He should be there for Passover."

Jerusalem, Malachi thought. It had been long time since he had visited the Holy City.

"Does this miracle worker have a name?" Malachi asked.

"Yeshua," Haran answered, "Yeshua of Nazareth."

That night the dreams were vivid. Through the darkness, Malachi could just barely make out the shape of two doors. With his arms outstretched, he slowly felt his way toward them, shuffling his feet from fear of tripping over some invisible obstacle. The air around him was stifling, as if the sun were standing right beside him. A deep sadness settled in Malachi's heart. He tried as he walked to shake off the feeling, but the utter hopelessness was so intense that Malachi had to fight the urge to simply lie down and die.

As he pressed forward, a thread of light became visible between the two doors. When he finally reached them, the doors opened, and Malachi was flooded with an intense feeling of joy. The air, that had been so hot and foul, was now cool and fresh. The feelings of sorrow had vanished as well, and, in their place, was so much peace that his head began to swim.

Without hesitation, Malachi stepped inside. In front of him were rows of wooden benches, with an aisle running up the center. At the end of the aisle was a small set of stairs that led up to a large wooden altar. Iron candelabra as tall as a man stood on either side of the altar like guards, their candles glowing a soft flaxen hue. But their light paled in comparison to the light that shined from just behind the altar. Hanging on the wall was a four-foot-high gold cross, etched to look as if it were made of wood. Malachi wondered who would give a symbol of death such an honorable place to rest. The cross gave off an intense glow, as if it were made of light.

As Malachi inched closer to the stairs, he saw shards of glass piled on top of the altar. When he reached the top step, Malachi could see that the glass had been in the shape of something at one time. Seeing the shattered pieces rekindled the feelings of sorrow and loss in his heart. Malachi buried his face in his hands and began to weep for Theudas.

Then a trumpet sounded from above the sanctuary. Malachi looked up just in time to see a beacon of light shine down on the pieces of glass. The intensity was more than his eyes could take. Malachi looked away, shielding his face from the brightness with his arm. After a few moments, the trumpet blast faded, and the beam of light was gone. A broad smile spread across Malachi's face. Where the shards of glass had been stood a three-foot-high statue of a dog.

Malachi let out a sigh of relief. Then reaching out, he gently ran his hand down the back of the statue. Instantly, a tingle shot through his hand and settled in the inscription on his skin. Malachi pulled his hand away and inspected his arm. The inscription began to smoke, the letters raising up on his skin. Panic struck Malachi as he frantically began rubbing it. But the inscription kept smoldering and then, to his horror, burst into flames.

Malachi flailed around trying to put out the fire burning his forearm. Then he took too many steps backward. In a flash, he tumbled down the stairs. A sharp pain rang in his head when he hit the bottom step. After that, everything went black.

When he awoke, Malachi found himself not in the strange sanctuary, but safe on his mountain, in his bed. Malachi sat up and stretched. As the sun crept across the dirt floor of his cave, he massaged the back of his head. The pain from his dream lingered there, refusing to fade with the morning. Glancing down at the inscription on his arm, Malachi was surprised to see that the lettering had indeed been swollen, but was slowly returning to normal.

For the next hour, Malachi tended to his usual morning ritual of exercises. But he couldn't shake the dream from his thoughts. Was it a sign? Perhaps, he contemplated, Haran was right.

Malachi gathered his walking stick and bedroll. Once again his hope was pointing him to the holy city. But this time, he would be seeking a Prince of Peace, not a king of war.

CHAPTER 15

"This cannot be the same city!" Malachi exclaimed. He could not believe how much had changed since the days of King Josiah. The only thing that had not changed was the entrance gate, near the Hinnon Valley. But, once inside, Malachi was visually assaulted by the vast amounts of gold and white stones used to adorn the buildings.

"It is indeed the same, Malachi," Haran said solemnly. "Herod the Great pillaged many a Jewish citizen to create this monstrosity. And that buffoon, Antipas, has lived in spoiled lavishness at the cost of the people as well."

Malachi shook his head in disgust. "Why has no one done anything about these atrocities?"

Pointing down the street, Haran responded, "*They* are the reason."

In the distance, Malachi saw two soldiers, wearing strange leather armor, long-laced sandals, and flowing red capes. Each man carried a long spear and a sword attached to his side.

Malachi raised an eyebrow. "What are those?"

"Romans," Haran said under his breath. "Our captors, and our slave masters. They are the real power in Jerusalem, some say the world. Herod Antipas is simply a puppet for Caesar. It is the hope of many, that this Yeshua you seek will seize the throne and deliver us from the tyranny of these invaders."

Malachi, Haran, and his family continued on until they reached the entrance of the temple. The main courtyard was bustling with merchants selling sacrificial animals and money exchange tables, along with throngs of people from every corner of Israel and beyond.

Haran motioned to his family to continue on. He then turned to Malachi. "This is where we must part ways, my boy," he said, sadly. "When I present my sacrifice in the temple, I will pray to Yahweh that He will one day redeem you."

Malachi's eyes grew wide with confusion. "Why must we part here?"

"Because," Haran answered, "your birth will not be in the records. The temple priests will not let you beyond the courtyard of the Gentiles. It is just as well. I understand the man you seek prefers the company of Gentiles anyway."

Haran and Malachi said their goodbyes. Then Malachi watched his old friend walk through the gateway that led to the Jewish-only inner courtyards. Malachi took a deep breath and looked around. Everywhere he turned, there was wall-to-wall people.

Like a spawning fish, Malachi slowly waded through the sea of people and animals that filled the Gentile courtyard. The smells of dung and body sweat made his eyes water. He desperately looked for a place to break free from the crowd. Then he spotted a dove merchant near the outer wall. The merchant made eye contact then, smiling, waved Malachi over. Malachi nodded then began to make his way toward the table.

As he approached the merchant, the man called out to him. "Sacrificial doves here, my young friend!"

Malachi stopped and turned his head, trying to avoid the merchant's rotten breath. The stinky little man was barely five feet tall and dressed in several different animal skins. Other than a left eye that constantly looked off in the opposite direction of where it should, the merchant appeared as average as any other man.

"I am not looking to buy any birds," Malachi said, wrinkling his nose, "but I am in need of some information."

The merchant pulled two small turtle doves out of their wicker cages. "These," he said as he stepped around to the front of the table, "are my finest doves. I will give them to you for a very fair price!"

Malachi shook his head. "I told you, I am not interested in buying birds—"

"Come now!" the merchant shouted, shoving the birds in Malachi's face. "Just look at them! Finest doves in all of Israel, and a bargain at four shekels for the pair!"

"Balthazar!" a creaky voice shrieked from behind a stack of bird cages. "You are a cheat and a swindler! Stop lying to that boy!"

"My mother," the merchant muttered nervously, pointing behind him, "pay her no mind. She is old and does not realize the price of merchandise goes up over time. Now, about these doves—"

Malachi grabbed Balthazar by the front of his clothes then turned him around so his back was to the crowd.

"Let me be clear," Malachi said through clenched

teeth, "I said I want some information, and that is all I want!"

Then his nose was filled with the faint scent of perfumed oil. The aroma was familiar, but one he had not smelled for many years. He looked up and saw a hooded woman standing in the middle of the passing crowds. She stared at him intensely, her dark eyes willing him to remember her.

He averted his gaze for a moment, his mind racing, trying to place where he had seen the woman before. When he looked back, she was gone. Then, without warning, she reappeared directly behind the dove merchant. The woman smiled seductively, revealing a long pair of needle sharp fangs.

"Zilpah?" Malachi gasped, letting go of Balthazar. Malachi shifted his gaze to the dove merchant in disbelief then back to the woman. But again, she was gone.

Malachi shoved Balthazar aside and broke into a slow run. *How can this be?* he thought. Quickly, he weaved in and out of the crowds, scanning every woman's face. When he reached the main entrance of the temple, Malachi realized she had vanished. Defeated and confused, he slowly walked back to Balthazar and the doves.

"My friend, are you well?" Balthazar asked, as Malachi approached the table. "You look as though you have seen a ghost."

"I…uh…I think I may have," Malachi said, shaking his head.

"Listen, about before," Balthazar said. "I am sorry. If I have the information you seek, it is yours, no charge."

Malachi thanked him then asked if Balthazar had seen

the man known as Yeshua of Nazareth.

"You are looking for the Rabbi Yeshua?" Balthazar laughed. "Get in line, my young friend! After the mess he made around here, I would not be surprised if half the nation was looking for him!"

"What do you mean?" Malachi asked with a frown.

"He was here in the courtyard a few days ago," Balthazar snorted, "turning over the money tables, pushing people away. Cracking a whip and going on about how we were all defiling *his Father's* House. Why would you want to seek him out?"

"That is my business," Malachi said sternly.

"Okay, okay!" Balthazar replied, putting his hands up in mock surrender. "It is your business. I understand he and his followers are celebrating Passover in a home not too far from here." He paused, looking up at the sky. "It is going to be dark soon. You should be on your way. Jerusalem is a big place and can be a dangerous city for young people at night."

"Thank you," Malachi said quietly, "but I have nothing to fear in the city." Then he turned, and walked away, absently leaving his bedroll and walking stick behind.

Balthazar watched with curiosity as the strange youth left the courtyard of the Gentiles. "Nothing to fear in the city?" he asked in amazement. "I wonder what he means by that." Perhaps it was nothing. Passover did bring all kinds of interesting people to Jerusalem.

Out of the corner of his eye, he saw a red cape moving through the crowd. Balthazar ducked behind the dove cages as an angry Roman sentry stormed by, the soldier's eyes feverishly scanning the vendors as he passed.

When the Roman was gone, Balthazar stood up and glanced down at the abandoned bedroll and stick. Perhaps this strange boy was his ticket out of Jerusalem. He decided to find out.

84

CHAPTER 16

The darkness of night draped over Jerusalem as Malachi maneuvered through the maze of streets that made up the holy city. Even though the sun had set nearly an hour ago, there were still hundreds of people in the streets—some looking for a place to sleep, and some already looking for a place to sleep it off. Malachi moved swiftly, making sure he avoided eye contact with the crowds he passed by.

When he reached the house, Malachi found himself filled with doubt. *What if Yeshua cannot help me?* he worried. *Or even worse, what if he won't?* Not ready for another disappointment, Malachi shook his head and turned to leave. Then the creaking of a door hinge pulled him back. Malachi turned and saw a man stumble out of the house and step out onto the street. His eyes were cloudy, almost corpse-like.

Malachi opened his mouth to call out to the sickly man, but stopped short as a dark figure emerged from the shadows. Malachi quickly stepped back and watched as the figure put an arm around the man and began to lead him back behind the dwelling.

For a moment, Malachi just stood still, unsure of what to do. Then fear gripped his chest. What if that man was Yeshua? What if he was in danger? With his mind made up, Malachi stormed past the door of the house and followed the two men into the small garden behind the dwelling. As Malachi rounded the hidden corner, he was stopped short by a monstrous scene.

The dark figure had a hold of the man by the back of his head. Facing the man, the dark figure leaned in, as if to kiss him. Then an animal-like growl erupted from this throat as the dark figure sank long fangs into the man's neck. Malachi gasped aloud. The creature looked up and focused on the sound, allowing the moonlight to illuminate its face.

Malachi's blood ran cold with hate. "*You!*" he yelled. "Why are you here?"

The creature released the man then casually wiped a stray drop of blood from his chin. "Half breed, it has been too long."

Ra pressed his lips against the man's ear and whispered. The man nodded silently and began to walk away.

"Wait!" Malachi called out, "Stop, where are you going?"

In three large strides, Malachi was in Ra's face. He grabbed Ra by the front of his tunic and shook him. "What have you done to that human?" Enraged, Malachi shook him harder. "Answer me, Egyptian pig! What are you doing here?"

With both hands, Ra gave Malachi a shove and stepped back. "I am here on business," Ra replied, straightening his clothes, "for my lord Lucifer. It is not your concern."

"I want to know what you said to that human!"

Malachi demanded, pointing his finger in Ra's face.

"The zealot Judas is not your concern, half breed," Ra said, with a defiant smile. "However, since I have you here, there is a small matter Lucifer wanted me to discuss with *you.*"

"He has nothing to say that I would want to hear," Malachi huffed.

"Do not be so sure," Ra said with a wink. "Lord Lucifer believes it is time for you to come home. After all your father Azazael has done for you, I would think you would want to honor him by taking your rightful place at his side." Ra paused and let what he had said sink in. "Simply declare Lucifer your lord and master, and by morning you will be reunited with your father. No more searching, no more trying to fit in. You will at last have a real family."

Malachi could feel the pull of Ra's proposition. After all, he had been alone for so long. Was this the answer he had been searching for all along? As he weighed his options, a faint voice pushed its way in from the back of Malachi's mind.

"Wait for a sign from God," it said.

Malachi closed his eyes and thought of Theudas. He thought about the old man who turned his back on his people so Malachi would live. The man whose last words, as he lay dying on the trade roads, were of love and hope. The man who never gave up hope in Malachi's redemption. In that moment, he knew what he had to do.

"What do you say, half breed?" Ra asked. "Shall I take you to your father?"

Malachi opened his eyes and glared at Ra. "My name

is Malachi Ben Sinai. And my *father*, Theudas, is dead. I say no." Malachi turned on his heel and started back toward the street.

"Where are you going, half breed?" Ra called out.

"I too, have business here," Malachi said over his shoulder.

Ra started after him then stopped. "It is too late for you to save him!" he yelled nervously. "The Lamb will be slaughtered, and you my friend, will still be *damned*!"

Malachi ignored Ra's warning. All that mattered now was that he find the zealot.

CHAPTER 17

"Wait," Malachi called out. "I just want to talk to you."

The zealot continued to walk down the narrow street.

Catching up, Malachi grabbed Judas by the arm. "Stop!" he yelled, spinning him around.

Judas stared blankly at Malachi, his expressionless face like a death mask. A small drop of drool trickled down his chin, getting caught in his beard like a cobweb.

"Please," Malachi said. "Where are you going? Are you a follower of the rabbi Yeshua? Can you take me to him?"

"Caiaphas," the zealot mumbled, walking away.

"No," Malachi said.

But it was hopeless. Whatever spell had a hold on Judas would not be broken by yelling. Malachi quickly decided it would be better to simply follow the zealot, and hope.

Judas rounded a corner and continued up the street that led back toward the temple. The pace was slow but, eventually, Judas led Malachi to the home of the high priest, Caiaphas. Malachi waited behind a large clay pot at the base of the steps, while Judas was inside. A few moments later, the zealot emerged, followed by a dozen temple guards. The sight of the guards startled Malachi.

Why would a self-proclaimed rebel like Judas align himself with temple guards? he wondered.

Malachi followed them, making sure he stayed several paces behind and out of sight. The trek took him through the entire city then out the temple gates that led to the Garden of Gethsemane. When he entered the garden, Malachi could hear hushed conversations from the people who were camping there. The guards' presence had caused quite a stir.

Judas and the guards stopped at a group of men a few yards ahead of Malachi. He edged himself a little closer then climbed into an ancient olive tree for a better view. From there, he could see the guards, poised just behind the zealot. He watched as Judas stepped forward and placed his hands on the shoulders of the man closest to him. Then he leaned in and lovingly planted a kiss on his cheek. When Judas took a step back, Malachi could see a single tear, glistening in the corner of the zealot's eye.

The kissed man's response cut the silence like a hot sword. "Friend, do what you came for."

Chaos exploded in the garden. The guards charged forward, ready to put their prisoner in chains, when out of nowhere one of the kissed man's companions drew a sword. Swinging it wildly, the man sliced off the ear of one of the guards. The injured guard screamed in pain, clutching the side of his head. The remaining guards immediately drew their weapons.

The kissed man raised his hands up to the guards and spoke. "Am I leading a rebellion, that you have come with swords and clubs to capture me? I preached every day in the temple courts, and you did not arrest me there." As he spoke, the kissed man walked over to the injured guard and knelt down. He reached out slowly and cradled the guard's injury in his hand. "But this has all taken place so that the writings of the prophets might be fulfilled."

With his last word, the kissed man pulled his hand away. To everyone's amazement, the guard's ear was completely healed. The kissed man smiled and patted the guard on the cheek then rose.

For a brief moment, everyone present stood silent, their eyes shifting back and forth from the guard to his mysterious healer. Malachi's mouth was agape in disbelief at the miracle he had just seen.

But the moment didn't last. The guards, regaining their senses, seized the kissed man and quickly chained him. Malachi watched as the kissed man's companions and the back stabbing zealot scattered like leaves in the breeze. When the temple guards finally left with their prisoner, only the once injured guard remained. He simply sat on the ground, shocked and silent.

Malachi waited several minutes in the tree, trying to process what he had just witnessed. Did this man really just heal a severed ear? Malachi hopped down from the tree and cautiously approached the guard.

"I saw what happened," Malachi said, crouching down next to the guard. "What is your name, friend?"

Eyes wide, the guard replied, "Malchus—my name is Malchus."

"Tell me, Malchus," Malachi quizzed, "why was that man arrested?"

The guard looked up at Malachi with blood shot eyes. "The high priests are afraid he will start a rebellion. If he is declared king, they could lose their authority over the people. They value the scraps from Caesar's table far more than the lives of the Children of Israel."

"Really?" Malachi asked, eyebrows raised, "but he seems so gentle. Tell me, friend, does this troublemaker have a name?"

"Yeshua…" the guard said, his voice trailing off. "He is Yeshua of Nazareth."

Malachi could feel the blood drain from his face. Perhaps the only person who could help him, other than Yahweh Himself, had just been arrested. Malachi leapt to his feet and broke into a sprint toward the city gates. All he could do was hope he was not too late.

CHAPTER 18

Amassive crowd had gathered at the home of the high priest, Caiaphas. The people were buzzing about the rabbi from Nazareth, and how the temple guards had arrested him. Malachi waded through the mob, trying to get closer to the door. Finally reaching the stone steps, Malachi positioned himself at the bottom, with a clear view of the entrance. If he timed it just right, Malachi knew he could grab the rabbi and whisk him off into the night.

The throng of people began to get restless. Theories about Yeshua's arrest began to circulate in the crowd. Was he trying to start a rebellion? What of these claims that he was the Messiah? A booming voice from inside the house answered all of their questions.

"He has spoken *blasphemy*!" the voice screamed in an infuriated tone. "What do you all think?"

Other voices chimed in dark unison, "He is worthy of death!"

Malachi fought back the urge to vomit. He knew enough about the laws of Israel to know that Yeshua was doomed. Fighting back tears, Malachi squeezed his eyes shut to calm his nerves.

"Just wait," he whispered.

The doors flew open. The temple guards and some of

the priests paraded Yeshua down the steps, and through the sea of people. The rabbi was badly beaten, his facial features already distorted and swollen. The crowd exploded with shouts and cries, some against the priests' decision, and others condemning the prisoner.

As Malachi stepped forward to make his move, Yeshua turned his head and stared right into his eyes. The condemned rabbi shook his head slowly. "Your battle has yet to come."

Malachi froze.

The bruised and bloodied face of the rabbi was full of love and understanding. As if He knew Malachi's intentions and was asking him gently to stand down.

Malachi dropped his hands down to his sides and stepped back into the crowd.

The angry mob began to break up, some following the guards to the prison, while the rest wandered off to find some other means of entertainment. But Malachi noticed that one man stayed behind. At the bottom of the stone steps, the lone man looked strangely familiar, his face twisted and overwhelmed with grief. It took Malachi a moment to realize where he had seen him, the garden.

Calmly, he walked down the steps and put his hand on the man's shoulder. "You were with him in the garden, were you not?" he asked quietly.

The man stood up and jerked away from Malachi's touch. "I do not know what you are talking about!" he barked, before stalking off into the night.

This was the same man who cut the ear off of a temple guard in defense of Yeshua only a few hours ago. Why deny him now? Malachi wondered. He watched the distraught man walk away as a rooster crowed faintly in the distance.

"I warned you this was going to happen," Ra said calmly.

Malachi looked behind him and saw Ra and Zilpah walking toward him.

"But you did not listen," Ra continued.

"Have you not done enough?" Malachi hissed through clenched teeth. "Why have you come here? To torture me further?"

Zilpah let out a giggle and glided up to Malachi. She put her arms around his neck, then lovingly nuzzled his neck. "It has been so long, my body has ached for you. Tell me that you missed me," she purred, running her fingers through Malachi's hair, "as much as I have missed you."

Malachi remained motionless, staring at Ra with disdain.

"The unfortunate events of the evening should be proof enough for you, that these humans and their God cannot give you what you need," Ra said. "Look what they do to the one they call 'teacher.' What do you think they would do to a half breed son of a demon like you?"

"It would be more fun to imagine what I could do to you, instead," Zilpah teased.

Malachi grabbed Zilpah by both arms and shoved her away. A deep growl bubbled up in her throat, as she flashed a pair of needle-like fangs.

Ra stepped in front of her. "That is enough, Zilpah. Give the half breed time to adjust to you. After all, you two love birds will have all of eternity to get to know each other." He turned to Malachi and sighed. "Her blood was delicious, but I am still not sure if allowing her to change was worth it. Zilpah can be…how shall I say?…quite a handful."

Malachi frowned. "Changed into what, exactly?"

"I cannot say," Ra answered, shrugging his shoulders, "I fed from her, and she did not die like the others. My curse has somehow been passed on to her. Although, I am most envious that she is able to walk in the daylight." Ra paused a moment, reflecting. "It has been nice having a companion. And even you must admit, she is a very beautiful creature. She is so full of…vitality."

"She is a monster, nothing more," Malachi fired back. "Just like you."

Ra chuckled. "Yes, well, you would *know*, would you not? But we can debate that another century. I want you to consider Lucifer's offer. The humans will never understand you the way we do. Come with me, let me reunite you with your real family. I will even give you Zilpah."

Malachi refused. "No. I made a promise to Theudas, and I intend to keep it. Besides, I am just as much human, as I am demon. Lucifer and my father will just have to accept my choice."

"*Fool!*" Ra spat. "You have no idea the pleasure and power you are giving up. Full-blooded demons would pay dearly for what you were freely given. There is nothing for you here!"

A small figure emerged from the darkened street, dragging several sacks and a long walking stick. Malachi closed his eyes and sighed heavily, as Balthazar, the dove merchant, approached.

"Master, I have secured a place for us to sleep," Balthazar said, bowing deeply to Malachi. He eyed Ra and Zilpah with a suspicious glare. "If you are ready to take your leave."

Ra put a finger to Malachi's chest. "This conversation is not over, Half breed." he said, "Sooner or later you will have to answer for denying the dark lord."

A sudden gust of hot wind filled the air with dust from the streets. Malachi closed his eyes and waited for it to pass. When he opened them again, Ra and Zilpah were gone.

Malachi turned and frowned at the dove vendor. He opened his mouth to speak, but Balthazar beat him to it.

"He was right about one thing," he said seriously. "There really is nothing for you here."

"H—how much of that did you h—hear?" Malachi stuttered.

"Enough to know your plan has failed. Enough to know that I was right to follow you all night long. The temple priests will condemn the rabbi and probably have him executed for heresy." Balthazar leaned closer to Malachi and whispered, "Do you really want to find out what would happen if word got out that there was a child of a demon loose in the holy city?" Balthazar paused for a moment, thinking. "What you need now is a change of scenery, my friend!" he declared, snapping his fingers. "Let us go far from these lands and make for ourselves a new life!"

Malachi crossed his arms in front of his chest and gave Balthazar a skeptical look. "What about your birds and that mother of yours?" he asked. "You could leave them so easily?"

"Well," Balthazar said, "she is not really my mother, and it is not exactly by choice that I must leave," he answered, nervously. "You see, we would both be leaving our old lives behind."

Stepping closer, Malachi crowded the merchant. "I do not believe you. What are you running away from?"

Balthazar put his hands up and stepped back. "Nothing! I mean, nothing really. I *may* owe a Roman sentry some money. But I cannot pay it, so, I am leaving. Really, it is for the best. After all, if he does not see me, he will not be pained by the loss of his coin."

Another heavy sigh escaped Malachi's lungs. Perhaps seeing a new land would do him some good. And maybe it was time for a new strategy.

"Very well," Malachi said, "but, no more lies. When do we leave?"

A broad smile spread across Balthazar's face. "I have bartered us passage to Rome on a merchant ship. It sails in the morning. But we will have to hurry, if we are to make the ship."

"Bartered?" Malachi asked suspiciously. "What do you and I have to barter with?"

"Relax, my friend!" Balthazar said, handing Malachi his walking stick. "We will be spending the next few weeks working on the ship in exchange for passage. Trust me. By the way, what is your name?"

Malachi shook his head and slung his bedroll over his shoulder. For some strange reason, he did trust him.

CHAPTER 19

Present Day

"Father Glass?"

Caleb rolled over onto his side, the sounds of his snoring drowning out his assistant's voice.

"Father Glass!"

Startled, Caleb bolted upright. With shaky hands, he smoothed his wild hair. Had he slept here all night, he wondered. With a yawn and a stretch, he stood up. It wouldn't be the first time that he woke up with the imprint of his office couch on his face.

"Good morning, Joan," he said, plopping down at his desk. Caleb absently grabbed the coffee cup he left from the day before, gave it a sniff, then, shaking his head, set it back on the desk. "You're here early. Services don't start until ten."

"Uh, Father," said Joan, "it's a quarter till."

Panic struck Caleb like a punch to the guts. "Are you kidding me?" he yelled, as he jumped to his feet. "No, no, no!" Frantically, he began rifling through drawer after drawer of his desk. Sweat began pouring down his face, dripping onto the contents.

"Father, if I knew what you were looking for—" Joan

began.

But, Caleb cut her off. "Sermon, I can't believe I forgot to write the damn sermon!"

Joan blinked in shock. She knew Father Glass had been off his game lately, but this was bad even for him. Calmly, she walked around behind him and began pulling a selection of books from the shelves on the wall. She set them on the desk in front of Caleb, then stepped back. "Okay, today you were gonna preach on Matthew, so I've pulled some books that deal with that Gospel," she said. "I'll go announce that services are going to be late. Say, thirty minutes?" She paused to check with Caleb. He had stopped digging through his desk and, instead, was just sitting, staring at her.

"Father Glass, did you hear me?" she asked sternly, "Is thirty minutes enough time?"

Then, a knock at the door grabbed both of their attention.

"Thirty minutes is plenty of time, Joan," a commanding voice replied.

Caleb and his assistant looked up to see another priest standing in the doorway. Father Roger Hall marched across the office. His long legs and broad shoulders gave him more of a soldier's gait than a humble man of the cloth. But he found that those qualities, coupled with his handsome face, helped to build confidence in his sometimes timid flock.

"Oh, thank Heavens, Father Hall," Joan said, smiling with relief. "I'll leave him in your capable hands."

While Joan rushed out to notify the congregation of the delay, Roger sat down across from Caleb. He reached into his front shirt pocket and pulled out a battered pack of cigarettes. Then he tapped one out, lit it, and closed his eyes. "Did you forget I was coming?" he asked calmly.

Caleb stared at Roger, his mouth hung open in surprise. "I thought you quit?" he said.

"I did," Roger answered, taking a deep drag. "It lasted a whole six weeks. Don't dodge the question, Caleb. What the hell did I just walk in on?"

Caleb's eyes darted around the room, looking for something other than Roger to concentrate on. Roger Hall had been his friend since seminary, encouraging him like a personal cheerleader, listening like a father, and, when needed, nagging like a wife. Caleb let out a sigh and shook his head. It was time to come clean. "Roger," he started, "I don't think I can do this job anymore." He looked into his friend's eyes, expecting to see an understanding face. Instead, he found no expression at all.

Simply nodding, Roger said, "Go on."

Caleb swallowed hard. "I feel hollow, Rog, like a huge piece of me is missing. When I stand at the pulpit and give my sermons, it's as if I'm teaching on literature, not facts." He paused for a moment then went on. "I don't hear God's voice at all. Instead, I keep having these weird dreams, and I'm forgetting the simplest things. I can't take the stress anymore!"

Roger stood up and began to pace the floor. "I knew when I first met you, that you were going to do great things for Christ. You know how I knew?" he asked. "Because you had suffered a great loss and turned to God for comfort. A person can't help others give their lives to Jesus without a testimony. You see, that's why you're here.

This is where the Lord wants you to be."

"No," Caleb argued, "this isn't for me at all. I don't feel God's presence. I don't get messages from Heaven that lead me to one person or another. He hasn't blessed me with any gifts of the spirit. God has abandoned me, just like my parents did."

Weeping, he buried his face in his hands, his shoulders keeping time with his sobs. Roger walked around the desk and stood behind Caleb. He placed his hand on the young priest's shoulder and squeezed.

"I never really wanted to do this, Roger," Caleb sniffed. "I thought priests were spiritually bullet proof. Like, nothing ever made them sad or angry. The collar was supposed to set me free."

Roger took a long drag off his cigarette. "Well," he said, exhaling a cloud of blue smoke, "the truth is, we are called to carry all of our own sorrows, plus those laid on us by our flock." He reached down into the waste-basket and pulled out an empty soda can. He dropped the smoldering butt into the can then returned to his seat. "The good news is that we also carry their joys.

"I believe you're where God wants you to be," he continued. "Why do you think seminary was so easy for you? I have never heard of anyone as young as you being ordained. For Heaven's sake Caleb, you're only twenty four!" he spouted, pounding his fist on the desk. "Clearly, He's preparing you for something great. That's why He cleared the path for you to be the priest in this church."

"Really? How do you know?" Caleb cried. "Did He tell you that? Because He doesn't tell me a damn thing!"

Roger shook his head. "Caleb, calm down. It's not that

you can't hear God, you're just not *listening* to Him!" He looked at his watch and frowned.

Easing, Caleb took a deep breath. "My thirty minutes are up, aren't they?"

"Naw," Roger replied, "we've got a few more minutes. Look, you're gonna sit this Sunday out, okay? I'll do the sermon, then tomorrow, we'll call the Bishop, and maybe get you some time off. All right?"

The young priest nodded, wiping his face on his sleeve. "Okay."

"Don't think about it anymore today," Roger said, heading for the door, "If you stop clouding your mind with worry, it'll be easier to hear what the Lord has to say."

"Maybe, that's what I'm afraid of," Caleb said under his breath.

CHAPTER 20

While the procession made its way toward the church altar, voices of all shapes and sizes belted out "Amazing Grace." Caleb glanced around nervously as he sang, feelings of anxiety burning a hole in his stomach. He climbed the steps to the altar, then stopped and bowed. He inhaled deeply through his nose, taking in the scents of lemon oil and incense that clung to the old wood. Turning to his right, Caleb stepped forward and positioned himself in front of the celebrants' chair. Roger followed next, then one at a time, assorted lay clergy took their places.

When the song ended, Caleb turned and faced the congregation. Opening his arms wide, he greeted his small flock. "The Lord be with you."

"And also with you," the people joyfully replied.

"Let us pray," he said, closing his eyes. "Heavenly Father, whose Glory it is always to have mercy: Be gracious to all who have gone astray and bring them again with penitent hearts and steadfast faith to embrace and hold fast the unchangeable truth of Thy Word, Jesus Christ. Amen."

Caleb and the rest of the congregation took their seats with the exception of one young woman.

"The first lesson," she said in a loud voice, "is taken

from the book of Genesis, chapter twelve, verses one through eight. Please follow along in your pew Bible."

Absently, the young woman tucked a stray lock of curly blond hair behind her ear then read her verses, exclaiming "The Word of the Lord!"

The parishioners answered "Thanks be to God."

Then she took her seat. For the next ten minutes, two other members of St. Bartholomew's Church stood up from their pews and read their assigned Bible lessons. Through it all, Caleb maintained a glazed expression.

Roger leaned over and gave Caleb a nudge. "Pay attention, Caleb," he whispered. "You need to go down and read the Gospel now."

While the congregation sang another hymn, Caleb stood and walked over to the altar, retrieved the book of Gospel readings, then walked down the steps and stood among the pews.

"The Holy Gospel of our Lord Jesus Christ, according to John," he said, holding the open book above his head.

Right on cue, the people responded, "Glory to You, Lord Christ."

With a shaky voice, Caleb began reading John chapter three. "…For God sent the Son into the world, not to condemn the world, but that the world might be saved through Him." He paused and held up the book. "The Gospel of the Lord."

"Praise to You, Lord Christ," replied the congregation.

As the organist played a slow song, Caleb returned to the altar, replaced the Gospels, then took his seat. Excited whispers floated through the air as Father Roger Hall stood and walked to the pulpit.

"Brothers and sisters," he began, "I'm blessed to be here with you all this morning. As you know, services started a little late today, so I promise not to drone on and on up here."

Roger smiled as several giggles and even some clapping erupted from the pews. Shaking his head, he began his impromptu sermon. "All of us remember the first Bible verse we memorized in Sunday school," he said. "Like most of you, mine was John 3:16, 'For God so loved the world, that He gave his only begotten Son. That whoever believes in Him shall not perish, but have everlasting life.'" He paused a moment then continued. "But as we grow older, many of us tend to forget what a true sacrifice God made for us that fateful day. We forget that Jesus died on that cross, so we wouldn't have to. We committed the crime, Jesus did the time." He paused again, letting his words wash over the congregation. "That's what I want to talk about today. Jesus came into the world, not to condemn it, but to save it. What does that mean to you?"

As Roger launched into a dissertation of the Gospel, Caleb leaned back in his chair and closed his eyes. *What does that mean?* he wondered. He didn't feel saved. If anything, he felt as if he were constantly running from some phantom from his past, the ghost of unfinished business.

Yawning, he opened his eyes and looked out at the congregation. As he eyed each person, a brief feeling of comfort settled over him. *There they are*, he thought, *sitting in the same seats every week.* The faithful sheep of his flock, coming to him every Sunday for guidance and inspiration. He wondered if they would be so trusting, if they knew he didn't share their enthusiasm. If they knew their priest's faith was in danger of slipping away. Suddenly, an unfamiliar face grabbed Caleb's attention.

The boy, barely eighteen, sat stoic in the last row of seats. He showed no emotion, but was clearly entranced by what Roger had to say. There seemed to be wisdom in his face, as if a wise old man were looking out through his youthful eyes.

Caleb stared at the boy for several minutes, willing him to look up and meet his gaze. Finally, the young man turned his head and peered right into Caleb's eyes. The intensity of the boy's stare made Caleb jump in his seat. He quickly looked away and tried to focus instead on a small wine stain on the carpet.

For the rest of the service, every time Caleb stole a glance at the young man in the last pew, the young man was looking right back at Caleb. By the time the congregation had finished the last line of "Onward Christian Soldier," Caleb had made up his mind. He had to meet this mysterious youth.

"Let us go forth in the name of Christ!" Roger called out at the end of the service.

He was cheerfully answered by a chorus of "Thanks be to God!" from the parishioners.

Then, as expected, the whole church began lining up to meet the charming priest. As Roger shook hand after hand, Caleb stood next to him, scanning the line for the boy from the last pew.

"Oh, Father Glass!" Pearl beamed, grabbing his hand in hers. "Why didn't you tell us you were going to have a guest speaker? What an inspiring message!!"

Smiling over at Roger, Caleb sighed. "Well, I like to keep you guessing, Pearl."

While Pearl rambled on, Caleb continued to search the crowd. *I couldn't have missed him, there's only one door in and out of the chapel.* Caleb's mind briefly drifted back to last Sunday, and his strange dream. He wondered if maybe he was going crazy. Maybe he dreamed the young stranger up. Caleb quickly shook off that notion. No, he had to be here.

Little by little, the line thinned, until finally only Roger, Caleb, and Pearl remained. Somehow, the boy had managed to elude him.

CHAPTER 21

"**W**ell, Caleb, how did you feel when you were giving the Gospel lesson this morning?" Roger asked.

The two of them had been sitting alone in the chapel for almost two hours. Roger had insisted they spend some time in prayer after the last of the congregation left. It was nearly four o'clock in the afternoon when the two men finally said their amens.

"I don't know," Caleb said. "I'm still convinced this job is not for me. It doesn't matter how many times I do it, I always get this uneasy feeling in the pit of my stomach."

"Well, that's natural," Roger said, nodding. "Some people have a hard time speaking in front of crowds. But that doesn't mean you aren't meant for this calling."

"I really appreciate you saving my ass today." Caleb sighed. "You know, with the sermon and all. I just wish I could figure out what's wrong with me."

Roger shrugged modestly. "We have been called to be leaders in the faith, Caleb. But sometimes even the greatest of leaders need help. We're gonna figure this thing out together, okay?"

Caleb nodded silently, keeping his eyes glued to the back of the pew in front of him. He trusted Roger with his life. If he said they would figure it out, then Caleb knew they would.

"Listen, I'm starving and need a shower," Roger announced, standing up. "I'm staying at that grubby little motel off the highway. If you feel like talking anymore tonight, I'm in room 206."

Caleb stood up and embraced his friend. "You've been so good to me over the years, Roger. I wish I could be needed by someone, instead of always being the one in need."

"That's where listening to God comes in, Caleb," Roger said, pulling away. "Tell Him you want to be needed, and He will send someone your way, I promise."

The two priests walked to the entrance of the church, where they said their goodbyes. As Caleb watched Roger's car pull out of the parking lot, a small tear crawled down his cheek.

"Well, Lord," Caleb said, peering up at the sky, "it'll probably be a disaster, but what the hell? I want to be needed!"

A mockingbird, perched on the power line above his head, sounded off with a chirp that reminded Caleb of a car alarm. Then quickly the bird flew off, soaring up over the church and disappearing behind it. He watched the bird fly away then walked back inside.

He locked the large wooden doors behind him then shoved his hands deep into his pockets and walked into the main chapel. As he passed under the archway that held up the balcony, Caleb thought he heard someone call his name.

"Father Glass?"

Caught off guard, Caleb whipped around, eyes wide. "Who's there?" he called out.

"Up here."

In the balcony stood the elusive young man from the morning service. His hair and eyes were dark and, coupled with his olive skin, Caleb guessed he was Italian or middle eastern descent.

"I was beginning to think your friend was never going to leave." The boy paused for a moment. "I hope I did not startle you. It was not my intention."

Caleb took a few steps back, his knees shaking. "My God. Have you been up there this whole time?" he stuttered.

"Yes," the boy replied.

A flush of red washed over Caleb's cheeks. That meant this stranger had been listening to him and Roger. His face burned with embarrassment.

"Please, Father Glass, do not be concerned. Your worries and your secrets will be safe with me," the young man reassured him. "I have worries and secrets of my own. That is why I am here."

"So, you're in need of a priest?" Caleb asked.

"Not just any priest," the boy answered. "You. I have been waiting a very long time to meet to you, Father."

"Okay," Caleb said slowly, raising an eyebrow. "What can I do for you…um…I'm sorry, I didn't catch your name."

"My name is Malachi," the boy said.

"Okay, great, Malachi," Caleb answered with a nod, "what can I do for you, Malachi?"

Malachi climbed up onto the balcony railing. "I need

you to baptize me—" His voice echoed. "—today."

Caleb put his hands up in protest. "Stop! First of all, you're scaring me, climbing on a hundred-year-old railing. And second, a person can't just come in off the street and get baptized! There are things that need to be discussed, commitments you have to be willing to make." He paused. "None of which can be done in one afternoon."

A panicked look struck Malachi's face for a second then faded. "You do not understand," he said. "It must be done today, before the sun sets. We have run out of time."

Caleb exhaled a deep breath. "Wait, what do you mean, *we*? Look, you said you've been waiting a long time, what's one or two more weeks?"

An animal-like growl erupted from Malachi's throat. Then, without warning, he leapt from the railing, sailing down to the floor and landing square on his feet. Caleb gasped as Malachi marched up to him, his face inches from the priest's. Caleb held his breath. Malachi's eyes glowed, like embers in a fireplace.

The young priest stumbled backward, catching himself on the edge of a pew. "What are you?" he whispered, "What do you want?"

"All I have ever wanted is to be a normal human," Malachi snarled. "To live as you do, to one day die and perhaps see Heaven. You are the man who can help me achieve those things. I, and one who was close to me, have sacrificed much to remove the curse of my father. His death cannot be for nothing."

Malachi took a step toward Caleb. Instinctively, Caleb put his hand out in defense. "T—that's far e—enough!" he stuttered. "This is a house of G—God, d—demon, you have no authority here!"

Stunned, Malachi froze where he stood. The glowing redness began to fade from his eyes as he spoke. "I am sorry, Father," he said gently. "I realize my appearance is frightening, but I assure you, you are in no danger. I need your help."

Caleb thought about the last thing Roger said to him before he left and felt all of the fear in his gut slip away. Was this an answer to his prayer? Caleb could see the hope emulating from this boy's face. He decided to take a chance and succumb to the voice.

"Tell me about the sacrifice." he said in a shaky voice.

Malachi motioned for Caleb to sit down. "We were in Rome," he began.

CHAPTER 22

64 A.D., Rome

"Where have you been?" Malachi asked, exasperated. "You said you would only be gone a few hours. It has been two days!"

The little dove merchant flashed a crooked smile as he set his bag down on the table. "Never mind all that. I want to show you something," he said in a giddy voice. He opened the bag, and turned the contents out onto the table. "I found this at that temple—you know, the one where they worship the bulls." Balthazar stuck out his tongue. "Disgusting!"

Hidden among the endless assortment of jewelry and coins Balthazar had pilfered from the temple was a simple rolled-up piece of metal. Malachi reached out and picked it up, turning the small-but-heavy object over in his hand. "What is this?" he asked with a frown. He closed his eyes, the beginnings of a headache setting in. "We need payment for rent, and you bring home a rolled-up piece of lead?"

"Did you know they actually stand under the carcass of the animal and let the blood wash down on them?" Balthazar exclaimed. "Ugh! It's bad enough all the pork they eat in this city, but blood baths?" Balthazar shook his head. "Unclean."

Malachi sighed. "Why did you bring home a rolled up piece of lead?" he asked again.

Balthazar shook his head, grabbing the trinket from Malachi's hand. "Not just a rolled up piece of lead," he said, rolling his eyes, "it is a spell, a magic spell."

Malachi slammed his fist against the table. "I told you I did not want you to do this! Now you will be damned, just like me. Why is that so hard for you to understand?"

Balthazar sat down next to Malachi and shook his head. "You could give me some credit, you know," he said slowly. "I have not done anything. Not without you beside me. Not without your blessing."

Malachi groaned with relief. "Sorry," he grumbled. "I was worried."

"We cannot avoid this subject forever, my friend," Balthazar said. "You and I have lived in this stinking city for nearly thirty years. I am getting old, you are not. And Nero's little henchmen are becoming more and more of a problem every day. I cannot help you find a cure if I am dead."

They sat in silence for a few moments. Malachi let the words of his friend sink in. Thirty years. Had it really been that long since they had left Jerusalem? To him, it seemed like only yesterday that they had stepped off the merchant ship and walked the long, paved road to Rome.

"Did you hear what I said?" Balthazar barked.

Malachi looked up. "What? No, I am sorry. You were saying?"

"I found someone who may be able to make me an

immortal, like you." Balthazar said. "I have arranged to see her tomorrow morning. The woman is named Saraphina. She makes these defixios, or 'curse tablets' for a living. Will you come with me to see her?"

Malachi looked into the hopeful eyes of his friend. "Are you sure this is what you want?" he asked. "I can tell you, to live forever is a lonely life."

"It will not be lonely!" Balthazar insisted. "You and I will finally have all the time we need to find a way to break your curse. I want this, my friend. Say you will stand by my side."

Malachi gave in. "You know I will. Who am I to turn my back on a most loyal companion?"

Balthazar's face lit up. "Trust me, after tomorrow, we will be free to explore the whole world for a cure. And you will no longer have to enter the arena of that God forsaken Circus Maximus. I do not know how you stand it."

Malachi rolled his eyes. Balthazar never ceased to amaze him. This little man, who regularly stole from Roman temples, cheated in street games, and once even pick-pocketed a Roman senator, disapproved of gladiators. Malachi shook his head, laughing.

"What?" Balthazar demanded. "What is so funny?"

"There is nothing to dislike." Malachi said, smiling, "I get to kill Romans for a living, and they love me for it! Besides, who are you to judge, a man who just robbed a Roman temple."

Balthazar waved a hand at him. "Bahh! I am doing them a service," he said in a gruff voice. "Denying their pagan gods tribute, means their gods will not answer their prayers. Perhaps the Romans will see the error of their ways and turn to Yahweh."

As usual, Malachi could not argue with Balthazar's strange logic. Over the years his smelly little friend had kept every promise he had made. Balthazar poured tirelessly over thousands of scrolls, looking for any shred of information on how to remove the curse. He traveled all over Italy and Greece, and even managed to sneak into the library at Alexandria, gathering information, talismans, spells—anything he thought would change Malachi into a full-blooded human.

Malachi got up from the table and stretched. Tomorrow was a big day, he reminded himself. The Roman prefect had promised a special event to be held at the Circus of Nero, instead of the Maximus. It was a good thing Balthazar's appointment was in the morning. Malachi didn't have to take to the field until noon. He lazily walked across the room, flopped on his bed, and watched Balthazar from there, as the man meticulously sorted his horde.

"Balthazar," Malachi called out gently.

The little dove merchant looked up from his loot. "Yes, my friend?"

"I have decided, tomorrow will be my last fight."

Balthazar stared at him a moment. "Really, why?"

"Because, after tomorrow, we will be different people," Malachi said with a yawn. "If this woman we are going to see does change you, we could be in danger. What if she tells someone? We already risk much, just being Jews in this city. So, after tomorrow, we need to leave Rome."

Balthazar scratched his beard. "You are right, I had

not thought of that," he said. "When you leave for the Coliseum tomorrow, I will get us transportation. Where do you want to go?"

"I do not know," Malachi said, nodding off. "Surprise me."

CHAPTER 23

T he cool morning air drifted lazily through the Roman streets as Malachi and Balthazar walked to the shop of Saraphina, the defixio writer. Malachi inhaled deeply as they passed the bakery, drinking in the scents of fresh-baked breads. Soon, the streets would be bustling with people buying and selling their wares which was a daily occurrence at the Regio, the marketplace at the east end of the Circus Maximus. Saraphina's shop was tucked quietly into a small space between a jewelry maker and a brothel.

When they arrived, Balthazar knocked twice on the rotting wooden door. There was no reply.

Balthazar flashed Malachi a nervous smile, then knocked again.

"You may enter," a voice moaned from inside.

Balthazar pulled on the rope door handle, and the two of them walked inside. At once, Malachi was assaulted by dense, stagnant air, stinking of blood and smoke. He put the back of his hand over his mouth, fighting the urge to gag while shutting the door behind him. Balthazar, who seemed unfazed by the odors, walked right in and sat down on a small stool. "Mistress Saraphina?" he called out gingerly. "It is Balthazar. I have come for our appointment."

The voice called out from behind a dirty brown curtain on the wall opposite the entrance. "Did you bring the immortal one with you?"

"Yes," Balthazar said. "Malachi is with me."

"Good," the voice replied. "Olisha will want him here."

Malachi glared at Balthazar. "Who is Olisha? Are you sure about this?"

"Sshh," Balthazar warned. "She will hear you."

The curtain parted and a small dark-skinned woman hobbled out, her arms full of scrolls. "Olisha is all powerful in the arts of black magic," she crowed, eying Malachi with contempt. Saraphina set down her load on the table next to Balthazar. "If anyone can do this thing you seek, Olisha can do it. Did you bring my payment?"

"Of course, I did," Balthazar said, standing up. "You can have half now, and the other half after the ritual is completed."

Saraphina nodded one time, her tattered dread locks falling forward, covering her eyes. She reached up and absently brushed the hair back, revealing a pair of deeply set yellow eyes. The contrast between her black skin and the paleness of her eyes was startling. Saraphina reached out her hand patiently, while Balthazar fumbled around in his sack. A few moments later, he produced another smaller bag and handed it to her. Saraphina opened the bag and peered inside. Satisfied, she tucked the bag into a hidden pocket in her skirts then motioned for Malachi and Balthazar to follow her behind the brown curtain.

The room, much smaller than the main part of the shop, was completely empty, except for candles mounted in each corner of the room and a single black marble pedestal setting in the center.

Saraphina pointed to the plaster wall to left of the curtain. "I need to gather some things for the ritual. You stand there and wait for me."

The two obeyed and watched as Saraphina began to set up the room. She outlined a large circle around the pedestal, using flour she scooped out of a small, red earthen jar.

This is the Veve," she said, without looking up. "Magic comes from the earth. We will draw on that power here."

When she had finished outlining the circle, Saraphina took one more handful of flour and blew it into the center. Then she placed a four-inch-long, paper-thin strip of lead and a single gold nail on the pedestal. She stepped back out of the circle, being careful not to damage the ring of flour. Finally, she set out four large candles at the top, bottom, and on each side of the circle.

Satisfied, she turned and faced Balthazar. "Come and stand beside me. I will begin the ritual."

Balthazar stepped forward, nervously wringing his hands. He looked back at Malachi and smiled. "This is for you, my friend," he said.

"I know," Malachi replied, "brother."

Balthazar's face lit up. He silently nodded then turned to face Saraphina. "Shall we begin?"

She raised her hands above her head and began chanting in a language neither Balthazar or Malachi had ever heard before. As the words crawled out of her mouth, the movements of her body became erratic, her hips pivoting in unnatural ways. Saraphina twisted her neck from side to side, while stomping out a dance around the Veve, always careful not to enter the circle or touch the flour.

She stopped, standing at the head of the circle. Then, she called out the last of the chant.

"*Yeke, Mar-ch-Allah, Kum Bha-la-Dya*, withdraw into the *light!*"

On her last word, the candles on the floor as well as the ones on the walls flared up, their flames turning from orange, to a deep blue. The dirt inside the circle began to swirl, as the ground opened up. Thick black smoke poured up from the hole in the floor, filling the room with the stench of sulfur.

"Something is wrong!" Saraphina screamed. "This is not how Olisha comes to her servants!" She looked over and pointed an accusatory finger at Malachi. "*You!* You are responsible for this! What creature have you conjured here?"

"Me?" Malachi exclaimed. "I am not doing this!"

Balthazar pointed to the hole in the floor. "I think something is coming!"

A cloaked figure slowly ascended up through the swirling smoke, the ground becoming solid again under its feet. For several agonizing minutes, no one spoke. Then, a dark, thundering voice boomed from the spirit.

"Who has summoned me?" it demanded. "What human dares to call upon Uphir?"

Saraphina bravely stepped forward. "It is not you I have called. Where is Olisha? Where is the dark goddess?"

The demon pulled back his hood, revealing his face. Large portions of his facial skin were gone, exposing the bones of his skull. Blue flames illuminated his hollow eye sockets like a pair of demonic lanterns.

Uphir roared in anger. "Do not demand answers from me, human! It was your spell that summoned me, Uphir, Chief Physician of Hell. Why have you called upon me?"

"I tell you the truth," Saraphina insisted, "be gone , demon! And send forth Olisha!"

The flames in Uphir's sockets began to grow. A growl rumbled from his throat, as he reached out a clawed hand toward Saraphina. Instantly, she began to choke. Saraphina's hands instinctively went to her neck, grasping at the invisible hands that were cutting off her air supply.

"You do not demand anything from me, human," Uphir growled. "If you did not summon me, you do not control me."

"Stop!" Malachi shouted. "You are killing her!"

Uphir turned to Malachi, and stared. Instantly, he dropped his hands, released Saraphina, then got down on one knee, and bowed his head.

Balthazar turned to Malachi and grinned. "Humph! I guess he belongs to you."

Malachi glared at Balthazar then stepped toward the circle. "Why do you bow to me, demon?"

Uphir stood and faced Malachi. "You are the son of our greatest general, Azazael. Your presence here must have caused my summoning. I am bound to serve you until you set me free. What would you ask of me, son of Azazael?"

"Just one thing," Malachi said. "Balthazar wishes to be immortal, as I am. Do you know a spell that can accomplish that?"

"Yes," Uphir answered. He looked down at the pedestal and gave a satisfied nod. "I have all I need right here. Step forward, human, and I will make you live forever."

Balthazar took a deep breath and stepped into the Veve with Uphir. The demon towered over him by more than two feet. That, coupled with the overpowering smell of sulfur, turned Balthazar's stomach. He swallowed hard and closed his eyes, trying to settle the queasiness.

Uphir took a hold of Balthazar, on either side of his head. "Eyes are the windows to the soul," he hissed. "I need yours to be open."

Balthazar opened his eyes. "Is this going to be painful?"

Uphir's flames once again began to rage in their sockets. He muttered a long incantation under his breath, his grip on Balthazar's head firm and steady. A green fog slowly began to creep out of Balthazar's mouth, swirling into a cloud then settling over the blank lead tablet on the pedestal. The demon released Balthazar then took a step back.

"The soul has been removed from the body," he said, admiring his work. "Now we must give it a new home. A safe home. Give me your hand, human."

Balthazar held out his hand. With his sharp claw, Uphir pierced Balthazar's finger then held it over the lead tablet, allowing a single drop of blood to drip onto it. Then he waved Balthazar back out of the circle.

"This blood is the link between your body and soul," the demon said. "Only with fire, can this bond be broken."

Relieved, Balthazar stumbled backward out of the

Veve, kicking up a cloud of dust and flour.

Malachi reached down and helped his friend to his feet. "You did well, brother," he whispered. "You will never know what your sacrifice means to me."

Balthazar patted Malachi on the back. "I meant it when I said I would always be there for you. You have changed my life, and I plan to do the same for you."

Uphir waved his hands over the lead tablet. Slowly, Balthazar's blood and soul began to soak into the strip of metal. When they were completely absorbed, the tablet began to roll up into a small, tight tube. The demon muttered another spell. Then he picked up the lead tablet and the gold nail and, with perfect precision, pushed the nail through the lead, sealing Balthazar's soul inside.

"A piece of chain, or leather," Uphir barked at Saraphina. "Now!"

Without a word, she hastily left the room. A few moments later, Saraphina returned, with a foot long piece of leather cord.

"W—will this d—do?" she stuttered.

Uphir took the cord from her without a word and quickly fashioned a necklace. When he was finished, the demon held out the finished defixio to Balthazar and smiled proudly. "Some of my finest work," he boasted. "I hope this fulfills your needs," he said to Malachi.

Malachi nodded. "It does."

Balthazar inspected the necklace. "It is amazing, I am here, and—I am in here! Fascinating!"

"You need to observe the rules," Uphir said abruptly.

"Rules?" Balthazar asked.

"Yes," Uphir replied. "Your soul is safe inside that

tablet and cannot be released without the proper spell. You are now undead, suspended in time. Although you are now immune to aging, injuries, and disease, your body can still be destroyed by fire, so you must be careful. But most important, keep your soul in a safe place. Do not let the defixio fall into an enemy's hands. They could use it to destroy you."

Balthazar turned and looked at Malachi. Then, he walked over and gently placed the necklace around Malachi's neck. "This is the safest place I can think of," he said, "Please say you will keep it for me?"

Malachi nodded. "Of course, I will." He glanced over at Uphir. "You have done what I asked," he said, "and are now free to go."

The demon bowed deeply, one hand behind his back, the other outstretched. "Thank you, son of Azazael. Any message for your father?"

"No," Malachi said, "there is no message."

Chapter 24

It was nearly noon when Malachi and Balthazar emerged from Saraphina's shop. The streets were alive with vendors, shoppers, and beggars alike. The two men weaved in and out of the crowd, making their way through the outskirts of town to the Circus of Nero, a gruesome coliseum perched at the top of Vatican Hill.

"You will meet me here in four hours with our travel arrangements?" Malachi asked.

"You actually think the fighting will be done in four hours?" Balthazar answered sarcastically. "What if Nero wants an encore?"

Malachi shook his head. "He will not. The emperor, in fact, will not even be attending the spectacle. The prefect arranged the whole thing. I heard he has some special event planned after the fights. I would not be surprised if he canceled our matches. He has done it before. Of course that means I will not get paid, but I do not care. Just be here in four hours, and we can finally put this city behind us."

They said their goodbyes, and then Malachi began his walk down the long stone corridor that led to the gladiator's quarters. He passed several burly fighters, each one eying him with contempt. Malachi was one of the more celebrated gladiators, his supernatural strength, agility, and youthfulness inspired everyone who attended the spectacles. But most of the paid competitors had nothing but disdain for him. Malachi's fame did nothing but cost them money.

He walked into the changing quarters and grabbed his leather armor and helmet. He didn't need them, but wearing them was necessary. Malachi worked very hard at making sure no one suspected he was only half human, sometimes going so far as to nearly lose a match. A tall sandy-blond fighter came up behind him and clapped Malachi hard on the back.

Malachi turned around and smiled with relief. "Nigellus," he said with a nod. "I did not know you were going to compete today. I heard that you had injured your back."

The nearly seven foot Nigellus threw his head back and laughed. " Ha! These Roman twats may have conquered my homeland, but not me! I will only be defeated when they put me in the ground."

Malachi chuckled at his friend. Nigellus had once been a great warrior of the Gaul but was sold into slavery after the Romans came. He'd paid for his freedom years ago, but Nigellus loved killing Romans too much to leave. For him, the war would never be over.

"Is Ferox fighting today?" Malachi asked.

Nigellus nodded. "Oh yes, the great Ferox is in the first round. And as usual, he is stomping around here like he is the emperor. He even went to Pollux and asked to fight one of us instead of the condemned."

"What did Pollux say?" Malachi asked, eyes wide.

"He said maybe," Nigellus answered with a shrug.

"You know how he is about money. If one of his paid gladiator's die, it cuts into his profits. Personally, I hope I get a crack at him. Ferox needs someone to put him in his proper place."

The roar of the crowd above them erupted, shaking the wooden beams that ran across the low ceiling and sending a rain of dust down on Malachi and Nigellus. A short, dark-haired man came clambering up to them, his breathing heavy and labored.

Nigellus looked down at him and smiled. "Ah, Pollux, we were just talking about you."

"I have no time for that forked tongue of yours, Nigellus," Pollux snapped, wiping the sweat from his red face. "You and Malachi are wanted in the arena."

Without another word, Pollux walked away, in search of the rest of his line-up. Malachi and Nigellus looked at each other and laughed. As they headed toward the ramp that led up to the arena, they heard Pollux yell, "Make me some money, you dogs!"

They both shook their heads and kept walking.

Malachi and Nigellus each got into one of the two lines that formed on the ramp. A small boy walked the line, handing a sword to each gladiator. Another boy followed and painted a red X on the back of every other man in the two lines. So, it would be a game of chance, Malachi thought, as the boy slathered the letter on his back. Xs versus non-Xs. Malachi glanced over at Nigellus. He had an X too. A wave of relief washed over him. He did not want his last battle to be against his friend.

Nigellus turned and met Malachi's gaze. Then, with a grin, he pointed toward the front of the line. Malachi looked and saw Ferox, ten positions ahead—without an X.

Ferox, sensing eyes on him, turned back and glared at them. He drew a phantom line across his throat with his hand then pointed at them.

"He is mine, Malachi," Nigellus said, grinning.

Malachi shrugged his shoulders. "Have at him, my friend."

Trumpets blazed, instigating another applause from the crowd. Slave girls, wearing simple white tunics, walked along the rim of the arena, throwing loaves of bread into the crowd. Then the massive iron gates swung open, signaling the gladiators to enter the arena. Two by two, twenty of the fiercest warriors from the great Circus Maximus marched to the center of the Circus of Nero, their helmets and swords gleaming in the afternoon sun. When they reached the center, the gladiators turned and faced each other, waiting for the ringmaster to announce the details of the fight.

The excited Roman crowd rose to its feet as Pollux, doubling as the ringmaster, stepped up to the podium, which was positioned just under the emperor's royal box. The fat, red-faced man raised his arms up, signaling for the crowd to be silent.

"Agrippa, the great Prefect of Rome, has arranged for your entertainment today. We will have a battle between the greatest warriors who have ever graced the Circus of Nero!" he began. "A contest of strength, a battle to the death. Citizens of Rome, who will be the victor? Xs, or non-Xs?"

The crowd began to shout out the names of their

favorite gladiators. Malachi looked across at Nigellus, his expression concealed by his helmet. But even with the obstruction, Malachi knew Nigellus was smiling ear to ear. He loved to hear Romans cheer for a man who killed Romans.

"Gladiators," the ringmaster continued, "turn and face the prefect."

In unison, the twenty men turned and faced the royal box. Then, raising their swords into the air, they chanted together, "We who are about to die, salute you!"

Agrippa leaned forward and absently waved his hand.

"Let the battle begin!" the ringmaster shouted.

Instantly, the two lines began to attack each other. The roman crowd erupted as the first gladiators were cut down. Within moments, the sounds of the dying and the smell of blood was thick in the air. The carnage continued, as one after another, Xs and non-Xs slaughtered each other. Finally, after an hour, only three gladiators were still standing: Malachi, Nigellus, and Ferox.

"It is us against you, Ferox," Malachi shouted over the cheers from the crowd. "Face the prefect and ask for mercy!"

"Never," Ferox sneered, "I will win the day, after all, look what I am up against, a boy, and a rotten, stinking Gaul!"

Malachi and Nigellus looked at each other in disbelief. He actually thought he could win?

"Nigellus—" Malachi nodded, stepped back, and planted his sword in the ground. "—he is all yours."

Nigellus ran his hand across his face. "You have had this coming for a long time."

"Yes, I have," Ferox replied. "When I kill you, I will dedicate your death to the Roman Legions who died bringing Roman superiority to your diseased culture."

They both let out war cries and rushed each other, the clanging of their swords wafting up through the stands. Ferox swung wildly, chipping off a piece of the blade from his sword. The flying metal launched straight into Nigellus's face, cutting into his eye.

Blinded, he dropped to one knee, feverishly trying to dig out the foreign piece of metal.

Ferox, seeing his chance for glory, made his move. He delivered a swift kick to Nigellus's mid-section, sending him sprawling to the ground.

"It looks as though I am going to win," Ferox laughed as he kicked him again.

Nigellus reached down into the ocrea strapped to his leg and fished out a small knife. "And just wait until you see what you have won."

With all the strength he could muster, Nigellus struck, burying the knife in Ferox's foot.

The big Roman roared as the pain sent a shock wave up his leg.

Nigellus stumbled to his feet then planted a huge right hook to Ferox's cheek.

Ferox stumbled backward and landed hard.

With his one good eye, Nigellus scanned the ground until he found his sword. He quickly retrieved it then gazed up at the VIP box.

Thunder from crowd erupted as Agrippa rose from his seat. He held out his fist, his thumb extended, so that it rested parallel with his lips. His eyes scanned the endless faces of the mob then, smiling, gave the signal: thumbs down.

Nigellus glanced down at Ferox and grinned. "Beg for your life," he said.

Ferox pulled himself up on his knees and glared defiantly at Nigellus. "You would not dare kill me," he answered. "I am a citizen of Rome, and you are nothing but a rotten stin—"

His words were suddenly cut off with one swipe of Nigellus's sword. The crowd got back on their feet as Ferox's head went sailing through the air.

Malachi and Nigellus walked together back to the center of the arena and faced the royal box. Out of the corner of his eye, Malachi looked over at Nigellus and smiled. "Was it worth it?" he asked.

"Killing a Roman always is," Nigellus answered, winking with his good eye.

"The winners," the ringmaster called out, "are the Xs! As a special reward for your magnificent victory, the prefect wishes to honor you with a rare opportunity."

Nigellus sighed. "Why do I feel like we should be worried?"

Malachi nodded in agreement. "Because we probably should," he muttered.

CHAPTER 25

Trumpets blared as, once more, the large iron gates opened. Four Roman guards marched out onto the arena field, leading a single prisoner. Behind him were a hundred or more people, both noble and common. The women sobbed, while the men shouted angrily. The gates under the royal box opened, and two more guards came out, dragging a large wooden cross. The procession stopped in the center of the arena, next to Malachi and Nigellus. The prefect stood and approached the edge of the royal box. As he opened his mouth to speak, a man from the procession below began to shout.

"Tell us, Agrippa, Prefect of Rome, what evil has Peter done?" he shouted bravely. "Tell the people of Rome!"

Agrippa leaned against the edge of the royal box and looked down. "Silence!" he shouted back. "This man, Simon, the one called Peter, is guilty of godlessness! A crime punishable by death upon the cross!"

The crowd in the stands, smelling blood in the air, began cheering as the guards marched Peter over to the cross, lying on the ground a few feet away.

"Gladiators," Agrippa called out, " witness the crucifixion of another *filthy* Christian! Take comfort in knowing that your beloved government is going to great lengths to ensure that these criminals do not infect the whole of Rome with their evil! This is our beloved Emperor Nero's special reward for you," he said, motioning to the condemned, "a ringside seat as we dispense Roman justice."

Malachi and Nigellus looked at each other nervously then quickly bowed to the prefect.

"And now," Agrippa said, "does the condemned have any final words?"

Peter stepped forward and looked up at the Prefect. "Yes, I do." He turned around and faced the people who had followed him into the arena. "You men," he began, "who are servants of Christ, men who have hope in Christ, remember the signs and wonders done through me by our Lord, and that He did them for your sake."

As Peter continued with his address, Malachi suddenly realized he had seen this man before. He listened intently, hanging on Peter's every word, trying to recall where they had met. Nigellus stared at Malachi for a moment then leaned over and whispered in his ear.

"Do you know this man?" he asked.

Malachi shook his head. "I am not sure. He seems familiar to me, but I cannot think of where I have seen him."

"Well, take care, my friend," Nigellus warned. "your concern for this man is showing. Guard your emotions, or you will end up on a cross beside him."

Malachi said nothing, entranced by Peters words. For the first time, in over thirty years, Malachi thought back to the night Yeshua was arrested. For weeks afterward, rumors began to circulate about the rabbi from Nazareth.

Officially, he was tried, convicted, and crucified. But many people believed Yeshua had risen from the dead, a radical theory that had continued to gain momentum over the past three decades. In fact, Yeshua had acquired such a large following that Nero began to fear a threat to his rule. There would be only one man on the throne of Rome, and so the executions began.

The guards got to the business of tying Peter to the cross. The sounds of the women weeping and Peter's prayers were the only sounds in the arena. As they were about to hoist him up, Peter shouted for the guards to stop.

"Executioners!" he called out. "I ask you to crucify me with my head pointed downwards, and not any other way. For I am unworthy to bear my cross in the same manner as the Son of God."

Gasps from the crowd echoed throughout the coliseum. The guards looked up at Agrippa and waited for his permission. The prefect grinned and nodded with approval. The pain would be much more unbearable that way.

Malachi and Nigellus looked away, while the guards struggled to flip the cross and Peter upside down. Sweat poured from Peter's face, as his breathing became more labored. Miraculously, Peter continued his prayers, to the dismay of the prefect.

"We now ask the undefiled Yeshua for that which you promised us. Though we are weak, we praise You, we thank You, and we confess You are Lord above all others. Glory is Yours now and forever! Amen."

The people standing in the arena cried "Amen!"

As Peter gave up his last breath, Malachi suddenly realized where he had seen him. He started to lunge forward, but Nigellus quickly grabbed him. Malachi glared at his friend, trying to pull away.

"Let me go!" he growled through his teeth.

"Malachi, stop!" Nigellus answered, holding fast. "You cannot help him now. I know all too well what happens when you become an enemy of Rome." He loosened his grip on Malachi's arm. "You remember him now, do you not? Why does his death trouble you so?"

"I tried to console him the night Yeshua was arrested," Malachi answered "Never have I seen such despair in a man before that night."

"You tried to console him?" Nigellus said, eyebrows raised. "Malachi, you are still a youth, that man Yeshua was executed over thirty years ago. You must be mistaken."

Malachi shook his head. "No, I tell you the truth. I was there."

Nigellus let go of Malachi's arm. Something in Malachi's voice told Nigellus that he was speaking the truth. "You are not of this world, are you?" he whispered.

"I am from somewhere in between," Malachi answered.

The ringmaster's thunderous voice suddenly filled the Circus of Nero. "I now declare the games over! Honored gladiators, you may exit the field."

Malachi and Nigellus both turned and bowed to the royal box then began a silent walk back to the gates. When they entered the gladiators' quarters, they were met with cheers and singing.

"They are cheering for you, Nigellus," Malachi said,

"the man who defeated Ferox."

Nigellus smiled. "You think so?"

"Watch this," Malachi said. Thrusting his sword high in the air, he shouted, "Nigellus, the victor!"

Gladiators and slave alike began chanting Nigellus's name. Two large men hoisted Nigellus up on their shoulders and began to parade him around the quarters. In the midst of the celebration, Malachi silently slipped out of the Circus of Nero.

When he got outside the entrance, Balthazar was waiting for him. He instantly saw something was wrong.

"What is it my friend?" he asked. "Did something happen?"

Malachi motioned for the two of them to distance themselves from the crowd exiting the arena. "The night before we left Jerusalem," Malachi started, "at the courtyard of the high priest, there was a man—"

"You mean Simon, the one Yeshua called Peter," Balthazar said. "Yes, I remember you told me of him. What about him?"

Malachi swallowed hard, fighting back tears. "We were divided into two teams. Our team was victorious. As a reward, Agrippa crucified a Christian on the field and had us stand there and watch."

Balthazar reached out and put a hand on Malachi's shoulder. "And that Christian was Peter." Balthazar shook his head, staring at the ground in dismay. "I am more sorry than I can express. Did he die bravely?"

"That is what is tearing out my heart!" Malachi cried. "Simon Peter died with more honor than I will ever know. To his last breath, he stayed true to Yahweh, he stayed faithful to Yeshua." He paused, wiping his face. "On the same day a great man goes to Heaven, I allow my only friend to condemn his soul, for *my* selfish pursuits!"

Malachi turned his back to Balthazar and began to slowly walk away.

Balthazar called out to him in a stern voice. "You stop!" he shouted. He stomped up to Malachi, grabbed his arm, and spun him around. "How dare you take my sins upon yourself? How dare you act as though you forced me into this decision? I told you, I did this for you because I wanted to. I am your only friend. You are *my* only friend. And wherever the Lord takes you, I will follow. You called me brother. I intend to honor the title."

Malachi stood frozen, stunned by Balthazar's words. He never realized how strongly Balthazar felt about him. Malachi could feel the tension of the day's events begin to wash away. He knew in that moment, that no matter what happened in this world, Balthazar would never leave his side. He smiled weakly and nodded his head. "You are right," he said calmly, "I acted stupidly. Will you forgive my self-pity?"

Balthazar flashed his wide smile. "Of course! Today is a new beginning for you and me. We will leave this rotting city behind us. Come, let us go and fill our stomachs and then find someone to give us a ride to the harbor. We sail in the morning!"

Malachi chuckled to himself then took one of the bags from Balthazar and slung it over his shoulder. Then the two men started the long walk back into the city. As they were walking, Malachi suddenly had a thought. "Do you think Peter made it to Heaven?"

"Are you kidding me," Balthazar snorted. "I would not be surprised if, when he gets there, they give him the keys to the gate!"

CHAPTER 26

The impatient clicking of Lucifer's claws against the stone table echoed in the great meeting chambers. He had called this gathering over an hour ago, but one of his key members had failed to show up. The dark prince stared down the length of the table, keeping his eyes locked on the face of his greatest general.

"Why did you not let me send one of my soldiers," Azazael muttered. "Instead of that buffoon? You sent a doctor to do a warriors job."

"Where is he?" Lucifer growled. "For his sake, Uphir had better show up soon, or never again!"

Azazael chuckled under his breath. He knew it had been a mistake to send that fool to Rome. Any of the others would have been a better choice. But since Rome was full of mystics, Lucifer sent Uphir, the Physician of Hell, to gather information from his human followers. The dark prince had special plans for the humans who called themselves Christians.

The stone doors of the meeting chambers swung open. Hastily, Uphir entered the room and then closed the doors behind him. He walked quickly to his seat at the meeting table and sat down. "My brother," he said, "forgive my lateness. I was unexpectedly detained."

Lucifer rose from his seat. All eyes were on him as he

slowly strolled down to where Uphir was sitting. When he reached Uphir's chair, he calmly placed his hands on the demon's shoulders. "Are we not superior to humans?" Lucifer said, massaging Uphir's shoulders. "Is that not the reason we are so easily able to manipulate them?"

"My brother, I—" Uphir began.

"So, of course, it was not some weak human who caused the great Physician of Hell to nearly miss a meeting with the Prince of Darkness!" Lucifer bellowed, digging his nails into Uphir.

Uphir stood up and faced Lucifer. "I was summoned!" he yelled, sticking a clawed finger in Lucifer's face. "Some filthy woman summoned me. So, they have more power than you give them credit for, brother!"

Lucifer stepped back, eyebrows raised.

"Saraphina, priestess to that bitch Olisha, botched the ritual and summoned me instead," Uphir continued. "It was fortunate for me that Azazael's son was there, or I do not know how much later I would have been detained."

Azazael quickly looked up. "My son? Why was he there?"

"His companion desired to be immortal," Uphir answered.

"And did you give him what he wanted?" Lucifer asked, smiling.

"Yes," the physician answered. "I had no choice."

Lucifer burst into laughter and walked back to his seat at the head of the table. He sat down then extended his hand to Uphir. "Did you at least bring me anything useful?" he asked.

Uphir reached into his cloak and removed a tiny

insect. He whispered a quick incantation. Then a glowing blue fog surrounded the bug like a force field. The fog drifted down the table, stopping in front of Lucifer.

The dark prince extended his finger into the fog and retrieved the insect. "Why have you brought me a flea, Uphir?"

Uphir smiled. "You wanted a vessel for Poreskoro's newest disease. I believe this flea is what you have been looking for. It is small, it breeds by the thousands, and it travels with rodents."

Lucifer nodded silently. Poreskoro, Lucifer's creator of disease, would love this.

"The Christians are growing in numbers every day," Uphir continued. "Your servant Nero is not getting the job done. The more he persecutes them, the stronger their faith becomes. A plague could easily wipe them out, and that flea is the perfect carrier."

"I stand corrected, brother," Lucifer said. "This was worth the wait. Bring in Poreskoro."

A servant soul, standing near the door, quickly opened it and stepped out into the hallway. Moments later, the sounds of hissing drifted in through the door as Poreskoro made his entrance. The demon leaders stood up in reverence as the spirit of plague slithered in on his snake-like tail.

"You sssent for me, brother?" Poreskoro hissed.

Lucifer held out his finger, displaying the tiny insect on the tip of his claw. "Uphir has found the delivery system for your newest plague."

Poreskoro's green eyes glowed with dark delight. "Thisss is perfect," he said, "I shall be able to ssspread my pesssstilence immediately with thisss."

"Not yet," Lucifer said. "I want to play around a bit longer with Nero. The cruelty this human possesses is most impressive. When I am ready, I will call on you."

Poreskoro bowed then, taking the flea, exited the meeting chambers.

"Uphir," Lucifer said calmly, "go back to Rome."

The physician let out a disgusted sigh. "What would you have me do there?" he asked.

Lucifer smiled. "Burn it. Bring the fires of Hell to Italy. When the Romans blame Nero, he will blame the Christians." Lucifer smiled as he imagined the human city ablaze. "Go, do it swiftly."

With the meeting over, the rest of the leaders left the chambers, leaving Lucifer alone with Azazael. They sat motionless for a few moments, both demons reflecting on the events of the day.

Then with a heavy sigh, Azazael broke the silence. "Brother, would not the plague be more efficient?" he queried. "I mean, if it is your intention to wipe out the Christian resistance, why are you playing games? Just send Poreskoro with the disease and be done with it."

Lucifer chuckled. "You think like a general, brother. Ordinarily, you would be right, but this is not an ordinary war. It is not enough to just destroy them. We must break their spirits as well as their bodies. This fire is just the beginning."

Azazael shook his head. "Then why create the pestilence at all?"

"In nine hundred years, the Roman territory, Londinium, will become an independent nation known as

Great Britain," Lucifer said. "In thirteen hundred years, it will be the center of commerce and trade. From there, we can send our plague all over the world."

"So, this Londinium will be our staging point?" Azazael asked.

"Not just a staging point, brother," Lucifer said with a smile. "England and all of the surrounding islands will be ground zero for the black death."

CHAPTER 27

Present Day

"He would turn out to be my closest friend for many years," Malachi said, absently clutching the pendant around his neck. "I miss him still."

Father Caleb sat cross-legged in a pew, spellbound by Malachi's story. Perhaps it was because Malachi was a spiritual being that Caleb could physically feel the sorrow, as if it were vibrating out from Malachi's body. The young priest reached out and put his hand on Malachi's arm.

"What happened to him?" Caleb asked.

Malachi shook his head and stood up. "That is a story for another day."

"But what about after you left Rome? You can't just leave the story unfinished like that," Caleb begged.

"There is no more time, Father Glass," Malachi answered, clearly annoyed. "I need to be baptized before the sun sets."

Caleb folded his arms defiantly. "Come on, we have time. You can spare a few more minutes-"

Malachi leapt over the pew and grabbed Caleb by the neck. Holding the priest in one hand, he slammed him against the wall. When Caleb realized that his feet weren't touching the floor, he fell into defeated submission.

"Enough!" Malachi growled. "I walked away from the only home I ever knew. I have buried every friend Yahweh ever blessed me with. You whine like a spoiled child because I will not tell you the ending of my tale when, deep down, you know the ending already. Balthazar was lost!" Malachi released his grip on Caleb's neck. He stood back while the priest pulled himself back into the pew. "I am sorry, Father Glass," he said quietly. "Forgive my anger."

"No, I'm the one that's sorry," Caleb said, rubbing his neck. "But, you know, Jesus is the only way to Heaven. You should've focused on Him."

"How was I to know that?" Malachi shouted. "He was condemned to die. They put Him on a cross! It would be centuries before I realized the mistake I had made." Malachi ran his hands through his hair. "I had a dream once about this church. I had that dream again after Balthazar was burned. That is how I knew that Yahweh had not abandoned me. I have been searching for you ever since."

Caleb nodded slowly. "Okay, I don't know what to think about all of this, but you win. What do you want me to do?"

Malachi knelt down in front of Caleb. "Father, I am ready to receive Holy Baptism. Please, will you perform the ritual?"

Caleb stood up and adjusted his shirt. Then he looked down at Malachi and smiled. "Yes, I will."

Malachi rose to his feet. He glanced over at the window near the door and was filled with dread. The last rays of sunlight had almost disappeared behind the horizon.

Caleb trotted up to the alter, grabbed a small vial of oil, a bottle of Holy Water, and a prayer book from inside a recessed cupboard in the wall. He bounded back down the steps and walked back to where Malachi was standing. He noticed a strange look had washed over Malachi's face.

"What?" Caleb asked. "What's wrong?"

"Something I had hoped I would not have to burden you with," answered Malachi. "Ra is here. I do not know how he found me this time. But once the sky turns black, he will be free to roam in the open." Malachi turned and looked gravely into Caleb's eyes. "And in order to prevent the ritual, he will kill you. Just as he has killed others before you."

For the first time in his life, a mixture of fear and excitement flowed through Caleb. "Wow, then I guess we'd better hurry, huh?" With shaky hands, Caleb opened the prayer book. He turned and faced Malachi, crossed himself, then began to read. "Blessed be God: Father, Son and Holy Spirit, and Blessed be His Kingdom, now and forever, Amen." Then with prayer book in hand, Caleb raised his arms towards Heaven. "Alleluia! Christ is Risen!"

The large wooden doors of the church blasted apart. The shock wave sent Caleb reeling backward in the aisle. Malachi, unaffected by the blast, clinched his fists, turned, and faced the door.

Ra stepped across the threshold, shards of splintered wood and stained glass crunching under his boots. Then he smiled as he held his arms out and tilted his head to

one side, as if to mock the crucifixion.
    "The Lord has Risen indeed," he said.

CHAPTER 28

R a planted a quick right hook to Malachi's chin. Malachi answered with a punch of his own to Ra's cheek.

"How many times have we been in this situation, half breed?" Ra asked. "Refresh my memory, I cannot seem to recall. Have I killed three or four of your precious human priests?"

Malachi roared with anger then broke into a run, tackling Ra. For a moment, the two rolled around on the floor like a school yard brawl. Finally, Ra kicked Malachi off, sending him sprawling.

"Poor human wretches! They all lost their lives because of your selfishness," Ra ranted as he circled Malachi. "All of them innocent blood on your hands." He paused for a moment, pondering some silent thought. "Except for the one in Scotland. I take back what I said before. That amateur had it coming."

Ra laughed as he reached into his waistband and pulled out his golden dagger. As Malachi's eyes fell on the small knife, the sight of it immediately filled him with fear and hatred. His reaction brought more smiles to Ra's face.

"Oh, so you remember The Soul Stealer." Ra smirked. "Good. A man should know the name of his killer."

Malachi jumped to his feet. "You are the only one who

is going to die today."

Like so many years before, Ra and Malachi exchanged blow after blow, each one still evenly matched with the other. Malachi stole a glance at Caleb and saw that he was still passed out cold. Ra seized his chance and quickly kicked Malachi's feet out from under him. Once again, Malachi found himself on his back, with Ra pinning him to the ground.

"Now, why does this feel so familiar?" Ra asked. "Oh, yes, this is how we met!" He leaned down and whispered in Malachi's ear, "Do you feel as sentimental in this moment as I do?"

Malachi squirmed and twisted under Ra's weight, but couldn't get him off. Ra dug his knees harder into Malachi's shoulders then pressed the blade of The Soul Stealer against his neck. Knowing he was beaten, Malachi stopped struggling.

"There, that is much better," Ra sneered. "Now, all you have to do is return to Hell with me, and I will let the human live. No more games, half breed. This time, my orders are to kill you too if you refuse."

An ancient rage began to churn up from Malachi's gut. His eyes began to glow a fiery red. He shook his head slowly, his gaze locked onto Ra.

"My soul belongs to Yahweh," Malachi snarled. "You go to Hell."

Ra nodded, a mixture of relief and satisfaction on his face. "Good, I was not looking forward to having you there as competition. Now—" Ra paused and licked his lips. "—show me your demon."

Malachi's vision began to cloud, as the demon half of

his soul began to take over. He could see himself transformed, ripping Ra's body apart with his long clawed fingers. Ra stood up then backed away from Malachi. He watched with morbid fascination as Malachi writhed on the ground. The sounds of bones popping echoed in the church as the sand dweller shape-shifted into a demon.

Within a few minutes, the ancient boy from the mountains of Israel was gone. With his father's curse now fully manifested, Malachi stood three feet taller than before. His golden olive skin was now a dull cadaver gray. Malachi's cheekbones strained against skin that was so taut against his skull he no longer had lips to hide the four inch fangs that filled his mouth.

But it was Malachi's wings that were his most impressive feature. Expanding from his shoulder blades, the massive wings were made of pure hellfire and spanned twelve feet on either side. The wings, coupled with his long sinewy body, made the demon Malachi a fearsome sight.

Stretching out his fervid wings, he took a step toward Ra and roared. His thunderous voice shook the very foundation of the church, shattering a stained glass window in the ceiling that served as a skylight. Ra stood his ground. He shifted the dagger back and forth from one hand to another several times before settling on the right hand. He then reached out with his free hand and beckoned Malachi closer.

"Come on," Ra said through clenched teeth. *"Come on!"*

Malachi leapt into the air, his fiery wings pumping to keep him up. When he had reached the pinnacle of the church's vaulted ceiling, the demon Malachi roared again.

"Feels good, does it not?" Ra screamed. "All the powers of Hell flowing through your body, the strength of a thousand legions at your fingertips? Too bad it will not last!"

With all the fury he could muster, Malachi descended upon Ra, swiping his long bony claws. But, the former god was ready. At the last moment, Ra somersaulted forward, regaining his footing directly under Malachi. Before he could react, Ra plunged The Soul Stealer into Malachi's chest. The demon Malachi reared back, flailing in the air and clawing at the dagger. Sulfurous smoke began to leak from the wound. Malachi closed his eyes and fell to the ground.

Ra stood triumphantly over Malachi, as his demon form began to fade away. Within a few moments, the creature was gone, leaving behind the remains of Malachi, broken and dying.

"You see," Ra said, as he reached down and yanked the dagger from Malachi's chest, "it should have been easy for you to defeat me, even kill me! But you would not listen to reason. You denied the power that was given to you, and now you are going to die. But before you do," he said, looking over at Caleb's still lifeless body, "you will get to watch one last priest go to his maker."

Ra walked over to Caleb. He grabbed the injured priest by the leg and began to drag him unceremoniously to the altar. Malachi could only watch as Ra lifted Caleb up and placed him on top of the altar, under a large gold cross. In quiet desperation, he looked up at the shattered skylight and began to plead with God.

"Yahweh," Malachi called out weakly, "I thought this was where You wanted me to go, but look at what I have done. The life of this human is more important than mine ever was. Too many faithful people have died trying to feed my selfish desire. Please spare him. I am willing to live without You, if it means that Caleb will *live*."

Once more, Malachi's thoughts drifted back to Balthazar. The only mortal to pay with more than his life, Balthazar never gave up hope that they would one day lift Malachi's curse. As Malachi began to fall into unconsciousness, he allowed himself to remember their days in Scotland. Exhausted, Malachi felt himself slip back in time.

CHAPTER 29

1591, North Berwick, Scotland

Balthazar stood silently, pools of evening mist swirling around his ankles. He stared off into the dense forest in front of him. His heart was heavy. What would Malachi think if he knew what Balthazar was about to do? The decision to summon a demon had not been made lightly. With the witch trials raging across England and Scotland, the world they had tried so hard to hide was now dangerously close to the light. Lifting Malachi's curse had become more important than ever. Left without options, Balthazar decided to seek a second opinion.

He pulled a small leather journal from his pocket. Flipping to a marked page, he began reciting the spell. The circle of flour he made in the moist dirt began swirl and sink. A blast of sulfuric smoke and a hooded figure rose up out of the hole. Balthazar covered his mouth with the back of his hand and stepped back. Quickly, he whispered a prayer of protection then called out to the demon.

"Uphir?"

A gnarled claw reached up and pulled back the hood, revealing the face of Hell's Physician. The blue flames in his otherwise hollow eye sockets flickered with amusement.

"Little immortal," Uphir growled, "why have you

summoned me after all this time?"

"I need your council," Balthazar replied. "We have exhausted all earthly options. Malachi wants to break the curse of his father. I have searched every written document, every myth, and have found nothing."

Uphir released a guttural laugh. "Have you?" he asked. "There are two options you seemed to have overlooked, little immortal. I am not surprised, given your limited capacity for knowledge."

Balthazar's eyes grew wide. "What do you mean? What have I overlooked? Please tell me."

"Why should I help you?" the demon asked. "There is no gain for me to be charitable to a sack of bones. Convince me, human."

The dove merchant tilted his head to one side. "Malachi is the son of Azazael," he began. "Surely, it would fair well for you to aid the offspring of your commanding officer. I assume there are accolades to be won, even in Hell?"

Uphir smiled. "It is true, the general would be pleased with me for granting the wishes of his most beloved son, no matter what he may want."

"So you will tell me what I need to know?" Balthazar asked.

"I will," the demon replied, "but it will cost you."

Balthazar raised an eyebrow. "What do you want?"

"Never mind the price," Uphir said, waving his hand. "I will take my fee when the time comes."

Balthazar swallowed hard. A deal with a demon. No Jew in his right mind would contemplate what he was about to do. In desperation, he nodded. "Agreed," he said.

"You of course understand how to use a scapegoat?" Uphir asked.

"Yes, of course," Balthazar answered. "Why?"

"You and Malachi must return to Israel," the demon answered. "Pray the sins of the father into a goat and send it into the wilderness. Azaz, the sin eater, will do the rest."

"You mean, that old myth actually works?" Balthazar exclaimed.

"It works," Uphir said, casually glancing into the trees behind the dove merchant. "You can trust me. I am after all, a doctor. Of sorts. Oh, and there is something else you will need."

Uphir reached out and placed his hand on Balthazar's forehead. A searing pain erupted in his skull. Balthazar grabbed the demons wrist and pushed his hand away.

"Uggh! What did you do to me?" he cried.

"I have given you a spell of revenge," the demon said. "It will only work once, so use it wisely. When the time comes, you will know what to do."

"Thank you," Balthazar said, "I must go now."

"Yes, little immortal, you have much to do," Uphir replied. "Give my regards to the general's son."

Without a word, Balthazar turned and began walking back toward the village. As the sulfur started to swirl under Uphir's feet, another figure stepped out from behind the trees.

"You will have to hurry if you want to catch him," Uphir said, as he descended into the portal. "That human is about to ruin all of your plans."

Zilpah looked down at Balthazar's foot prints and smiled.

"Over here," she called out.

Four men emerged from the brush and surrounded her. Zilpah pointed at the ring of flour on the ground.

"You see," she said, "It is just as I told you. He is a witch. I saw him with a demon. He cast a spell and conjured the beast right here."

The four men stared with nervous eyes at the ring on the ground. One bravely stepped forward, reached down, and gathered up a pinch of the substance. Cautiously, he brought it up to his nose and gave it a sniff.

"Smells like sulfur," he said, brushing his hand off on his pants.

"What are you waiting for?" Zilpah yelled. "Go back to town and arrest him."

Without a word, the men began to trek back toward the village. Zilpah watched them with a sly smile on her face. Everything was falling into place just as she planned.

"The magistrate will be eager to burn this one," she said.

CHAPTER 30

"Well, I dare say, that was one wasted trip," Reginald said with a snort.

The modest carriage bumped along the muddy stretch of road that led to North Berwick. Small homesteads dotted the landscape, the smoke from their fires reaching toward the heavens like mystic fingers. Malachi took in a deep breath, savoring the crisp Scottish air. He and Balthazar had made Scotland their home nearly nine years earlier, and its beauty had not disappointed. Malachi shifted in his seat, anxious for the warmth of his fire and the sound of his companion's voice.

"French," Malachi muttered, shaking his head. "Leave it to them to convert a house of God into a jail. Balthazar was right, we should have stayed here."

"Quite right. What with the pope fighting with France, and Spain acting as the puppet master," Reginald grumbled, "I am afraid for monasteries like Mont Saint Michel. But I must say, it was pleasant to be out from under the evil eye of Protestant England and the paranoid ravings of King James."

Malachi chuckled at the quick wit of his companion. When the *Discoverie of Witchcraft* was published in 1584, he and Balthazar made a point of meeting its author. In

Reginald Scot, they found a fast tongue, a sharp humor, and, most of all, a trusted friend. The country-gentleman-turned-member-of-parliament had become an invaluable source for all things "other worldly."

"You are right about paranoid," Malachi noted. "It has been difficult to continue our work. With the witch trials commencing right on our doorstep, it has become dangerous to even greet neighbors."

Reginald nodded in agreement. "Poor old James. I shall have gladness in my heart when all this devil worship and witchcraft business is over."

The two sat in silence for the remainder of the trip. Malachi's thoughts were scattered. It was rumored that Mont Saint Michel housed ancient writings on curses, writings that Balthazar had been eager to get his hands on. But chasing rumors was like chasing shadows, and Malachi discovered soon after his arrival, that the old monastery housed nothing more than cursed men and old monks.

Malachi closed his eyes and listened to the creaking of the carriage wheels as they crunched against the road. Reginald would be leaving in the morning to return to Kent. It saddened Malachi to see his friend go, but Reginald promised to finance a trip to the Vatican soon, and the idea of making a pilgrimage back to his old stomping grounds filled Malachi with anticipation.

In the distance, the faint sounds of shouting brought Malachi out of his daydream. He looked out the window of the carriage, and saw a small boy running toward them on the road. The driver stopped the carriage. Reginald poked his head out and called out to the youth.

"What is it, boy?"

"My lord, they have arrested a witch," the child panted. "In the woods, they say he was conjuring demons."

Malachi and Reginald looked at each other with concern.

"Whom did they arrest?" Malachi asked.

The boy stared at the ground, shaking his head.

"Boy!" Malachi shouted, "Whom did they arrest?"

"It was your servant, sir," the child answered, "It was Balthazar."

"My God, what has he done?" Reginald gasped. "Driver, get us to Saint Andrew's. Make haste."

Hooves pounded the road as the carriage sped toward the church. The shouting grew louder as the driver pulled the carriage onto the green. A crowd of angry men and fearful women surrounded the house of God, calling for the witch to be burned. Malachi and Reginald jumped out of the carriage and marched up to the entrance of the church. A burly man guarding the door stopped them before they could enter.

"I am sorry, sirs, but the magistrate is seeing no one," he said.

Reginald took a step closer to the man. "I am Reginald Scot, member of the House of Parliament. We are here to clear the name of the accused witch. Stand aside."

The man, now clearly unnerved, moved away from the door. "Begging your pardon, sir," he said. "Please go in."

Malachi and Reginald walked into Saint Andrews and headed straight for a small door next to the altar. Malachi knocked once then stepped inside.

"We have come to address the charges against my—"

Malachi stopped mid-sentence.

The magistrate leaned back in his chair and smiled. "Charges? It has gone beyond charges, half breed. The accused has been convicted."

"Malachi," Reginald said, pointing at the magistrate, "do you know this man?"

Ra stood up from behind his desk, the smile on his face broader than ever. "Oh, yes," he said, "he knows me very well. We are old friends."

Malachi clenched his fists. "What do you want, Ra? Why are you doing this to my friend?"

"Me?" Ra asked, "I am simply following the law handed down by our king. Your friend was seen conversing with demons in the woods. What kind of official would I be if I turned a blind eye to witchcraft?"

Reginald scoffed. "You know perfectly well you have no real evidence of the crime of witchcraft."

"Ah, but I do." Ra replied. "I have a witness."

The door creaked opened behind them. Zilpah sashayed past Reginald and Malachi, running her hand along the wall. The smell of her perfumed oil began to fill the room. Malachi could feel a stirring in his loins. It was that same musky, carnal scent that tempted him in King Josiah's palace. The same scent that taunted him in the courtyard of the gentiles. And now it was here. But something was different. Something tempting him that hadn't been there before.

"Malachi," Reginald said. "Are you listening?"

"I am sorry, what?" Malachi replied.

"This animal," Reginald barked, pointing at Ra, "says Balthazar is to be executed. Tonight! Are you going to allow this to happen?"

Ra chuckled. "Oh, he is going to allow it. Because if he tries to stop it, I shall accuse you both of being accomplices, and then, my dear Mr. Scot, you will die too."

"This is madness," Reginald bellowed.

"No," Ra replied, his eyes glued to Malachi, "this is business. Malachi knows what he needs to do in order to save his friend's life." Ra paused a moment. "Too bad his answer is always the same."

The door behind them opened again.

"Sir, we are ready," a voice said.

"Well, gentlemen," Ra said, straightening his coat, "it is time. Come and watch English justice."

"I will expose you," Malachi threatened.

Ra chuckled as he walked toward the door. "Will you? And just who do you think the people will believe? Me, their protector who was appointed by their sovereign , or you, the Jew who brought a witch to their town?"

Zilpah joined Ra at the door. She linked her arm in his and together they walked out, leaving Malachi and Reginald alone.

"How can you be so calm?" Reginald said.

Malachi reached out and squeezed Reginald's shoulder. "They will hang him," Malachi said. "We will cut him down and leave as soon as the crowd disperses."

"I do not understand." Reginald said with a frown.

"Balthazar," Malachi said, smiling, "is immortal like me."

CHAPTER 31

The whole town had turned out for Balthazar's execution. It seemed once again that Malachi would watch mankind gather together for a common cause, death. Mothers had bundled up even their youngest of children and brought them down to the Auld Kirk. No one was going to miss the chance to see the devil get his due, even in the middle of the night. Smoke from torches mixed with the salt from the ocean air, covering the old church with the stench of false justice.

Malachi and Reginald stood at the back of the crowd, just to the right of the gallows. Taunts and cheers began to echo through the darkness, as Balthazar was ushered out. Stripped down to his under garments, he was bound with rope and led like a dog on a leash. The procession passed the gallows and continued down the path leading to the far side of the church that faced the sea.

Malachi turned to Reginald, worry radiating from his eyes. "Where are they going?"

"I cannot say," Reginald answered. "but it appears they do not mean to hang him."

They followed the procession across the church grounds to a clearing of grass. A large stake had been erected and men were piling wood around its base.

"No," Malachi shouted, lunging toward the clearing.

Reginald grabbed him then spun him around. "What is it? I thought you said he was immortal."

Tears began to stream down Malachi's face. "He can be killed only with fire," he whispered. "I am such a fool. I should have known Ra would figure out Balthazar's weakness, and mine."

As Balthazar was being tied to the stake, Ra walked out and stood in front of the make shift bonfire. He held up his hand, signaling for the crowd to be silent.

"Loyal subjects of James IV," he began. "let it be known, that on this day, the thirteenth of October, in the year of our Lord, fifteen hundred and ninety one, justice was served in the form of disposing evil in our midst, by the burning of this witch."

The crowd cheered as Ra continued, pointing at the condemned. "It was by the power of The Almighty and the law handed down by our good king, that this practitioner of the dark arts was discovered. This man, Balthazar, was found by a witness in the woods, conjuring demons. So evil was this witch, that he even documented his spell casting in this journal," he bellowed, holding up Balthazar's leather book. "May God have mercy on his soul."

Ra placed the journal on the wood, then stepped to the side to make room for two men carrying torches.

"Light him," he commanded.

Malachi turned back and watched as the two men laid their torches at the base of the wood pile. "Reginald," he said, "can you get me out of Scotland?"

A pair of delicate hands ran up the sides of his arms, firmly kneading his muscles. As the scent of Zilpah's perfume filled his lungs, Malachi found he was unable to move or speak.

"Do not fear," she purred, "your friend is quite safe. I have entranced him, so we would be uninterrupted."

Zilpah's hands continued to explore Malachi's body, gliding along his chest and down his stomach. When she reached his groin, she slipped a warm hand into his trousers, grasped his manhood and squeezed. A gasp escaped Malachi's lips.

"I have waited a long time for this moment," she whispered, nibbling on his ear. "Since the first time we met, I have ached for you."

Malachi's eyes focused on the flames of the bonfire, while Zilpah continued to explore him. His mind, clouded by her spell, focused only on the lustful pleasure.

From the stake, Balthazar had a bird's eye view. The heat and smoke from the fire was slowly intensifying. He knew it would not be long before the flames would engulf him. Through the haze, Balthazar could see his life-long friend. A surge of adrenaline flooded his stomach as he watched Zilpah wrap her arms around Malachi and kiss him. Fear quickly turned to rage. Balthazar looked down at Ra. The time had come to use the only weapon he had left.

"Ra," he called out. "Since you deny me my companion, I deny you yours!"

A burst of thunder rumbled in the sky. The cheers of the crowd silenced, as a single flame from the bonfire shot out like a lightning bolt over their heads. The steady stream of fire wrapped itself around Zilpah like a snake, pulling her off of Malachi and dragging her through the crowd toward the bonfire.

Zilpah screamed in pain as the flame lifted her off the ground, suspending her directly in front of Balthazar.

"I hope you did not think I was just going to *let* you win." Balthazar coughed. "You and I are going to die together, and Malachi will be free."

The stream of fire whipped out and wrapped itself around the stake, engulfing Zilpah and Balthazar in a burst of flames.

Chaos broke out as the crowd scattered, many running for their lives in fear of the witch. Malachi's senses slowly returned. He looked down and saw Reginald sitting on the ground, his face full of bewilderment and confusion. Malachi reached down and pulled his friend to his feet.

"We need to leave," Malachi said abruptly.

"Quite right," Reginald said, dusting himself off. "I believe we have overstayed our welcome in Scotland."

The two made their way back to the carriage.

"Driver," Reginald said, climbing in, "take us back to the port. We are leaving."

The driver nodded, cracked the reins, and headed back toward the docks.

Malachi leaned back in his seat and stared blankly out the window. Through the sea of scattered people, he saw Ra, fists clenched, staring down at the carriage with eyes full hate and defeat.

CHAPTER 32

Present Day

Ra was almost giddy with excitement. He looked down into the now open eyes of Father Glass and flashed him a wicked grin. Seeing Ra's razor sharp canines, Caleb recoiled in horror.

"What is the matter?" Ra asked in a baby talk voice. "Never been somebody's dinner before?"

Caleb swallowed hard as Ra threw his head back and laughed. Caleb's eyes darted in all directions, searching for a weapon or a way to escape.

"Tell me something, dinner of mine," Ra quizzed, "I want a drink with my meal, so where do you keep the wine?"

Caleb raised a reluctant arm and pointed to the cupboard on the wall. "It's in there."

Ra pressed his hands together and bowed to the priest. "Ah, bless you, my son!"

He quickly grabbed the church communion wine and chalice from the cupboard. For the next several minutes, Ra worked in silence, pouring his wine, then meticulously placing the bottle, chalice, and The Soul Stealer on the altar next to Caleb. When he was satisfied with the presentation, Ra turned his attention back to Caleb. He bent over the trembling priest and inhaled deeply through his nostrils. "Mmmm, you smell delicious! The last time I drank the blood of a holy man was…" Ra looked over the altar down at Malachi. "Do you remember the last time I feasted on a priest?"

Malachi said nothing. Ra shrugged his shoulders and sighed. "Oh well, it does not matter. Let us just agree that it has been too long."

Ra took Caleb's head, cradling him in his arms like a newborn. His eyes grew cloudy, then black as the blood lust took over his mind.

"Do not fear," Ra whispered lovingly, caressing Caleb's exposed neck. "it will be over soon, just relax." Ra reared his head back then, like a viper, sank his teeth into Caleb's flesh.

The church building started to vibrate. The haunting tones of Heavenly trumpets began to fill the chapel. Ra released Caleb, his eyes scanning the ceiling, searching for the source of the noise. A beam of intense light streamed down through the broken skylight.

Shielding his face, Ra walked around the altar and stood at the top step. "Show yourself!" he bellowed at the light.

The trumpets blazed again as a winged figure dropped through the skylight, landing catlike on the chapel floor. The being stood stoic, his long sword glowing like the sun.

Through squinted eyes, Ra looked the being up and down with a smirk. "Church services are over, my friend, come back next Sunday."

"You have desecrated a holy altar in the house of The Most High," the being said, pointing the fiery sword at Ra,

"I have been dispatched by Him to right this wrong."

"Is that a fact?" Ra chuckled, "And who are *you* supposed to be?"

The golden-armored being took a step forward. "My name is Michael, Arch Angel and general of Heaven's northern army."

"Am I supposed to be afraid, angel?" Ra sneered. "I am known in the histories as a god!"

"You are known only as Ra—" Michael's voice rumbled like thunder. "—false god and bastard son of the fallen whore Lilith! The Most High has tolerated your presence for too long. The prayers and the cries of His chosen people will be answered. After this night, you shall walk the Earth, no more."

Ra clenched his jaw. "You are mistaken," he growled, "it is you who is not long for this world."

Michael stood firm as Ra bounded down the steps. When he was just a few steps away, Ra's hand instinctively went to his waistband. Then his face paled. The Soul Stealer was still on the altar. Ra looked over his shoulder for just a moment, but there was no time.

The Arch Angel smiled. "You seemed to have forgotten your weapon." he said. "No matter, it would not have saved you."

Michael took a step to the side.

There, behind him, stood Malachi. With a snarl, he once again began to stretch and change into his demon self.

"On this day," Michael said, "the darkness shall bring darkness into the light."

Malachi pumped his fiery wings, ascending high into

the air. Then like a bird of prey, he came down like lightning, snatching Ra by the neck with his clawed feet. He bolted back up into the air, through the broken skylight, and into the night sky.

"Join me," Ra bellowed. "It is not too late, half-breed! We can still rule this world."

Malachi roared then pitched Ra into the air. As the sun god began to fall, Malachi reached out and grabbed him by the throat.

"I do not want to rule this world," Malachi growled, squeezing Ra's throat. "This is the last time I will tell you no."

Ra's face began to swell, as Malachi's grip grew tighter. Within seconds, the sun god went limp.

Malachi roared again in triumph then released his grip on Ra, dropping him back through the skylight to the concrete floor of the church. Then his own strength began to fade. With what little energy he had left, Malachi descended back down into the church. He stumbled slightly as he landed then fell backward, losing consciousness.

Without a word, Michael walked over to where Malachi lay. He knelt down beside him and made the sign of the cross with his thumb on Malachi's forehead. A rush of air filled his lungs and Malachi immediately opened his eyes.

"Do I live?" he asked weakly.

"Yes, you live," Michael said with a warm smile. "The Most High has heard your prayer, Malachi. Caleb has been spared."

A tear ran from the corner of Malachi's eye. "Yahweh

be praised."

Caleb slid himself off the altar and slowly walked around to the top of the steps. Holding onto the railing for support, he watched with surprise and wonder as the Arch Angel Michael with just a touch, healed Malachi's wounds. Then, a groan caught his attention. Caleb's heart skipped a beat as he watched Ra pull himself to his feet. As the sun god stumbled toward Michael and Malachi, Caleb looked around desperately for a weapon. Seeing The Soul Stealer laying on the altar, Caleb didn't hesitate. He picked up the dagger by the tip of the blade and threw it. "God speed," he whispered.

The dagger sailed through the air swiftly, nailing Ra square in the back. The sun god screamed in pain, reaching behind himself and trying to pull out the blade. Swirls of black smoke began to pour from Ra's wound. Then the floor opened up, and dozens of decayed human arms reached out, grabbing at his legs.

"*No!*" Ra raged. "It is not fair—*Half-Breeed!*"

His cries fell on deaf ears. The arms took hold of Ra and, like his mother so long ago, hauled him down through the swirling hole in the floor. Then, as quickly as it had opened up, the hole closed, leaving only The Soul Stealer and the smell of sulfur behind.

CHAPTER 33

"Well done, Father Glass," Michael applauded. "The Most High has blessed you with a good, strong arm."

Caleb smiled weakly as he stumbled down the altar steps and then slowly limped down the aisle. When at last he was standing beside the Arch Angel, Caleb's strength faded away. "I'm so sorry, Malachi," he said, flopping down on the floor next to him. "I should have listened to you." Caleb shook his head in apologetically. "I almost got us both killed."

Michael reached down and pressed his hand against the two puncture wounds on Caleb's neck. "May the Lord bless you and keep you, Caleb Glass. The Lord make His face to shine upon you and be gracious to you. The Lord turn His face toward you, and give you peace." When he pulled his hand away, the bite marks were gone.

Caleb touched his neck, his eyes wide with amazement. He took a quick inventory of the rest of his wounds and found that Michael had healed them all. Caleb looked up at the angel, a relieved expression on his face. "What about Malachi?" he asked, shyly. "Can we still perform the baptism?"

Michael nodded silently. Then, on a bended knee, he held out his hands and gazed up through the broken skylight. A thin beam of golden light shot down from the black sky into Michael's hands. Malachi and Caleb watched as the light pooled in the angel's hands, swirling and solidifying into two shapes. When the thread of Heaven's light faded, Michael held a crusty piece of bread in one hand, and a wooden chalice in the other.

He spoke softly as he rose to his feet. "Malachi Ben Sinai, son of Awan, rise and face me."

Malachi stood up.

"And you, Father Caleb Glass," Michael said, "come and take your place beside him."

The angel handed Caleb the chalice and the bread. Then he turned to Malachi and crossed himself. "Do you renounce Lucifer and all evil spirits and all evil powers of this world that rebel against The Most High God?"

"Yes, I do," Malachi answered.

"Do you renounce your own sinful desires that pull you away from The Most High God?"

"Yes," Malachi answered again.

"Do you turn to Yeshua, the Messiah, and accept Him as your Savior?"

Malachi nodded solemnly. "I do."

"Finally," Michael asked, "will you promise to obey Him and put your whole trust in His grace and love?"

"With all that I am," Malachi said, his eyes glimmering with joy.

Michael turned to Caleb. "Will you be responsible for Malachi?"

"Yeah," Caleb stuttered, "I mean, yes, with God's help."

Michael took the chalice from Caleb. Then he passed

his hand over the rim, muttering a prayer under his breath. Slowly, the chalice began to fill with water. Michael dipped his fingers into the water then made the sign of the cross on Malachi's forehead.

"I baptize you, Malachi Ben Sinai, in the name of the Father, of the Son, and of the Holy Spirit. Your soul has been spared the burdens of Hell by the sacrifice of Christ. Amen."

Caleb and Malachi echoed with amens of their own, and then for the first time in his life, Malachi made the sign of the cross.

"Now," Michael said, "let us celebrate the redemption of man, in the breaking of the bread."

Michael took the bread from Caleb, bit off a piece, then handed it to Malachi who did the same. Afterward, Malachi handed it to Caleb, who took the rest. The angel once again passed his hand over the rim of the chalice. The water began to swirl inside the cup, its color changing from crystal clear to a deep burgundy red. Michael raised the cup to his lips and drank. As with the bread, he then handed the chalice to Malachi, who in turn handed it off to Caleb.

As the wine warmed his belly, Malachi felt a burning sensation on his arm. He looked down, and saw the inscription left by his father so many centuries before, begin to glow and smoke.

"What is happening to me?" Malachi exclaimed, panic brewing in his eyes.

The heat from the fire quickly spread, engulfing Malachi from the inside. He cried out, dropping into the fetal position, as the pain ripped through his body.

"You gotta stop this!" Caleb shouted at Michael, crouching down beside Malachi. "Something's wrong!"

Michael reached down and grabbed Caleb's arm, pulling him to his feet. "No, we must let the blood of the Lamb reclaim his soul."

Caleb stared at the angel, confused, "What?"

"Malachi is the son of a human woman and a fallen angel." Michael explained. "His father's curse was passed to him in the conception, like the nephilim before him. The Most High God is lifting the curse. Baptism with fire. We must not interfere."

Caleb and the angel stood silently and watched as Malachi writhed in agony, flames lurching from his eyes, as if Hell itself were trying to escape. Finally, after several minutes, the fire diminished and the pain began to subside.

Exhausted and soaked with sweat, Malachi pulled himself into a sitting position on the floor. "It is gone," he said, panting. "I can no longer sense another presence inside my head. For the first time, I am free." He looked up. "Thank you, Yahweh."

"My work here is completed," Michael said smiling.

Malachi stood up on shaky legs and held out his hand. "I thank you, Michael," he said, "but, may I ask one more thing of you?"

Michael nodded. "Of course."

"Please, will you translate this inscription on my arm? My fa—" Malachi paused. "Azazael told me it was a gift. What did he mean by that?"

"Oh, yes," Michael said, "as I recall, he told you to stop looking for a sign and start looking for The Most High Himself." The angel paused for a moment, then continued. "He was telling you to look for Yahweh in the flesh, to look for the Messiah. He knew, even then, that the only way to spare you from Hell was Yeshua. Nobody comes to the Father any other way."

"And the inscription?" Malachi asked.

"A promise," Michael said, "that any man can receive redemption from the Messiah. It is from the book of Matthew, chapter eight: 'Lord, I am not worthy that you should come under my roof, but only say the word, and my servant shall be healed.'"

Malachi took a deep breath. He understood what Azazael meant when he had called it a gift. His father had given Malachi something that he himself could never hope to attain: forgiveness and mercy.

"So, am I a human now?" he asked.

The angel shook his head. "Not quite. You are still the offspring of an angel. Though you will remain an immortal, it is by The Most High's blessing that you will now enjoy the privilege of judgment." Michael stretched out his massive wings. "Your journey is just beginning, Malachi Ben Sinai. Do not squander the gift our Lord has given you. Peace be with you both."

Caleb and Malachi stepped back as the Arch Angel Michael pumped his wings and began to lift off of the ground. Just before he reached the broken skylight, Michael stopped.

Caleb," he called out.

"Yeah?"

"You are exactly where the Lord wants you. He has faith in you, and He loves you."

A bright light beamed down through the skylight into

the church. Caleb and Malachi both turned away, shielding their eyes. Then, as quickly as the light came, it was gone, and Michael with it.

CHAPTER 34

The afternoon sun filtered its way down through the trees, casting a collage of shadows on Caleb's back. He wiped the sweat from his forehead then pressed the last handful of dirt around the bush he was planting. Satisfied, he stood up and stretched his back. It had been four days since the incident in the church. But in spite of the twenty thousand dollars it was going to cost to repair the inside of the chapel, Caleb was finally happy.

"Father Glass!" a voice boomed from behind him.

Caleb turned around and smiled as Pearl Watersen walked into the freshly planted garden.

"Hey! Good afternoon, Pearl," Caleb said, wiping his hands on his shirt. "What brings you to the church on a Thursday?"

"Oh, Father, I just had to come as soon as I heard." Pearl exclaimed. "I just can't believe the police haven't caught the hooligans that vandalized our beautiful chapel! Why, if my Harvey were here…"

Caleb gathered up the gardening tools while Pearl rambled on. He was relieved that the police had adopted the "vandals" theory on their own. Caleb wasn't ready to explain what really happened.

"…and that's all I'm going to say on the matter."

"Well, thanks for stopping by, Pearl," Caleb said,

"unless there's something else I can do for you?"

"Well, Father, I wanted to tell you," Pearl said, taking Caleb by the hand, "something seems different about you. That sermon Father Hall gave last week must have had quite an effect on you. Anyway, I—" Pearl paused.

A young man came walking up, pushing a wheelbarrow full of landscape rocks. Pearl eyed the youth suspiciously, as he parked the load next to the garden.

"I got the stones you asked for, Father," the young man said. "If you do not mind, I would like to go back to repairing the pews. I am pretty sure I can have them finished before Sunday."

Pearl cleared her throat. "Father Glass, aren't you going to introduce me? I don't believe I've ever seen this boy before."

"Oh, yeah," Caleb said quickly, "Sorry, uh, Pearl Watersen, this is Malachi. He came here a few days ago looking for work. Turns out he's pretty good with a hammer, and it'll be a lot cheaper to pay him to do the repairs around here than a contractor." Caleb nervously turned to Malachi. "Malachi, this is Pearl Watersen, one of St. Bartholomew's church's most dedicated parishioners."

Malachi bowed deeply. "It is an honor to know you."

Pearl blushed. "Well, what a pleasant boy! And so handsome." Pearl looked Malachi up and down, her eyes landing on a strange tattoo etched into his right forearm. She raised an eyebrow, then reached out, grabbed Malachi by the wrist, and turned his arm to get a better look.

"What strange writing," she muttered, running her fingers over the words. "this isn't any language I've ever seen. What does it say?"

Caleb eyed Malachi cautiously, waiting for his response.

"Few people have seen this language written down," Malachi said. "It is very old. The words are a reminder to the wearer that the Lord watches over us all, and no matter how long you must wait, do not lose hope, for God answers the prayers of the faithful."

"That's a beautiful sentiment!" Pearl beamed. "But I can't say I approve of tattoos."

Malachi rolled his eyes. "Well, I was in a different place in life when I acquired it."

Pearl looked him up and down again with a serious expression.

"What is it?" he asked, searching her face. "What do you see?"

"You seem like an old soul to me," she replied. "A young man of the world."

"You have no idea," Caleb muttered under his breath.

Malachi shot Caleb a glaring look.

"Well, I must be going," Pearl declared. "The Yarn Barn is having a sale on fabric."

Caleb and Malachi watched the old woman get into her car and drive away.

"She's right, you know," Caleb commented. "You sorta do have an old soul."

"Yes," Malachi said with a sigh, "but a saved one."

EPILOGUE

Lucifer gazed out the large stone window that overlooked the grounds of his palace. The smell of Hell and rotting flesh wafted into the room on the winds. He closed his eyes for a moment, savoring the stench and intense heat. *How could anyone hate this place?* he wondered.

"So, your son chose humanity," Lucifer said, still staring out the window. "I imagine if you had a heart, it would be broken."

Azazael remained silent, lounging in a large overstuffed chair. He knew the dark prince had more to say.

"Are you satisfied with this turn of events?" Lucifer asked, turning away from the window. "Knowing your son will not be standing beside you in battle, knowing that he will fight *against* us when the time comes?" Lucifer sat down in the chair behind his desk and waited for Azazael to answer him.

"My son has always been free to make his own choices, brother. Just like every human," Azazael said, flatly. He stood up and walked to the door of the chambers. The demon opened the door, then turned back around.

"The real question is, are *you* satisfied with this turn of events?" Azazael strode out the door, slamming it behind him.

Lucifer reached down and stroked the long hair of a young girl lying on the ground next to him. Instantly, the girl arched her back then sat up and rested her head on his knee.

"I could understand turning his back on his father," Lucifer said to the girl. "since I myself did the very same thing. I sympathize with his independent desires. But to refuse an eternity with you—"

Instantly, the girl hissed. "When will I get my vengeance against the human? And the half breed, when will he finally belong to me?"

"My loyal Zilpah," Lucifer cooed, still stroking her hair, "soon. Let Malachi get comfortable in his new life. When he lets his guard down, I will send you."

Zilpah purred seductively, nuzzling the dark lord's thigh. She reached up and slowly began unbuckling Lucifer's belt. "I am yours, my lord."

Then Lucifer leaned back in his chair and smiled, his black eyes focused on the door. "No, brother," he said with a moan, "the devil never is."

ACKNOWLEDGMENTS

There are countless people to whom I owe a great deal. Without their knowledge and willingness to take an unknown like me under their wings, this book could not be possible. I am grateful to John Brantingham and his wife Ann, for championing me, mentoring me, and for simply being honest. Their influence and guidance have been indispensable, and I am humbled by their willingness to be a guide for budding authors. I would also like to say thank you to Bonnie Hearn Hill and Christopher Allan Poe, two phenomenal writers, who also moonlight as cheerleaders for those of us who want to break into the mysterious world of writing. Finally, I would like to thank my first fan, Arianna Guzman, who read The Sand Dweller when it was in its infancy, loved it, and never stopped hoping it would one day be in print. She is my muse and inspiration; I truly believe a piece of her light is imprinted in this book.

To my family, thank you for your tireless support. You never stopped believing in me. I could not have written this book without you. To my husband Lyle, thank you for being you. For your patience and your encouragement. For your love, I am eternally grateful.

Heavenly Father,

Thank You for all of the wonderful people You put in my path to make this novel a reality. I pray that You will Bless their lives with joy and happiness. I lift them up to You, that You will continue to use them to be a Blessing to others, and that You will fulfill their every need, as You always do for me. In the name of the Father, and of the Son, and of the Holy Spirit, one God, now and forever.

Amen.

www.ingramcontent.com/pod-product-compliance
Lightning Source LLC
Chambersburg PA
CBHW061442210726
48287CB00007B/2317